SLEEPOVER

A STEAMY SINGLE DAD ROMANTIC COMEDY

SERENA BELL

JMG
JELSBA
MEDIA
GROUP

1

SAWYER

"It's a shithole."

Brooks stands on the sidewalk outside my new place, arms crossed.

"Thanks," I tell my brother.

"Well, it is."

I sigh. "That's the point. I'm supposed to fix it up."

"Well, you've got your work cut out for you."

Typical Brooks. Doesn't mince words, doesn't apologize. Most of the time, those are great traits in a brother, especially for a guy like me who's zero bullshit. But every once in a while I wish he'd beat around the bush or drop a white lie, especially when it comes to the house I'm going to be living in for at least the next few months with my eight-year-old son, Jonah.

Brooks has a point, though. The roof shingles are peeling, there's enough moss up there that I think a tree is starting to sprout, and the house desperately needs a paint job—which I'm pretty sure also means some of those siding boards are going to need replacing. The yard is overgrown, a miniature suburban jungle.

The good news is, the more work I do on the house and landscaping, the less rent I pay.

The bad news is, for the first few months at least, Jonah and I are going to be living in a dump. And I've seen the inside. It's not a lot better.

A car pulls up to the curb behind the Penske truck I rented for this move. It's Brooks's friend Chase, with Jonah in the backseat. I can see Jonah through the window, his too-long hair shadowing his face as he leans over my cellphone, playing a video game. Chase tosses words over his shoulder to him, and Jonah replies. Knowing my son, he's saying, *I'll be there as soon as I finish this game.* Those are the words most often uttered in my house, besides, *C'mon, Dad,* really?

Chase gets out of the car and ambles toward us. "It's—got promise." He eyes the house like he's looking hard for something that would make his words true.

I raise an eyebrow at Brooks, like, *See, that's how it's done.*

Brooks shrugs. "I tell it like it is. No lube for you, asshole."

"You are such a dick."

"We share fifty percent genetic material."

"You were definitely adopted."

"Can you two quit it and come unload the truck? I told Liv I'd be back for dinner." Chase's arms are crossed.

Brooks rolls his eyes. "Wouldn't want to do anything that would keep Chase from having boring sex."

Chase laughs. "Spoken by a guy who has no idea what it's like to have the best sex of your life every fucking night."

That used to be me. A plentiful supply of reliable—and often great—sex. Terrific, now I'm horny and sad. It's so weird what'll still set me off, almost two years after my wife's death. Some days I'm fine, and others . . .

It didn't help that Brooks and I spent all of yesterday packing up the house where Lucy and I lived together. I thought her parents had taken most of her belongings—the ones I hadn't held onto and hidden away—but as I filled boxes, I kept finding her stuff. A sock of hers clinging to the guest towels. A binder she'd assembled with pages she'd ripped out of magazines and catalogs—recipes, photos of rooms she liked—

So many fucking things she never got around to.

If I've learned anything in the last two years, it's how to put one foot in front of the other. That's what I did yesterday, and that's what I do now. "Chase is right. Let's get this fucker done."

Of course, Jonah chooses that moment to exit Chase's car and come running up to us. *"Dad,"* he chastises.

"Sorry. Let's get this *thing* done."

Doesn't have the same impact.

Jonah pauses, and I watch, wincing, as he takes in the house, no doubt comparing it to our old house, which, while smaller, was in great shape. *"Dad,"* he whines.

"Don't start, Jo."

"It's a dump."

Brooks puts his arm around Jonah. "It has a lot of promise."

Chase snorts quietly.

"We're going to fix it up until you won't recognize it, bud. You and me," I tell him, looking down at his pale, sullen face, framed with a fall of straight black hair. He has Lucy's eyes, bright blue, and my chest aches.

"Why do we have to move?"

"You know why, bud. Remember, I explained? It was time for Nonna and Pops to move back to Florida"—my parents had come to stay long-term after Lucy's death, to help us out —"and that catalog, The Reclaimed House, wants my furniture, and so we needed to be closer to Gram and Gramps so they can watch you while I build. We'll have enough money by the end of this year to buy an even nicer house than our old one, near Gram and Gramps. And I'll let you help pick it."

"I know, but . . ." Jonah wrings his hands, a habit he started after Lucy died. It's painful to watch. I touch my fingers to his and he stops.

If Luce were here, she'd know how to get him to break the habit.

Of course, if Luce were here, he wouldn't do it.

"Come on, Champ," Brooks tells Jonah. "Let's find the boxes that go in your room and we'll get you set up."

For what it's worth, that's typical Brooks, too. No one worked harder in the weeks before and after Lucy's death to try to make things easier for Jonah.

Over the next couple of hours, there's not much conversation as Brooks, Chase, and I unload the truck, stack boxes, and do our best to arrange furniture. Brooks, true to his word, spends most of the time helping Jonah unpack. After a while, Jonah loses interest and begins exploring the backyard, and then making forays along the sidewalk to check out the rest of the neighborhood, which is a lot nicer than the house we're living in. I'm pretty sure the people who lived here the last three years didn't do any upkeep at all.

"Stay where I can call you," I caution him.

Brooks holds my phone out to me. I'd left it on the kitchen counter. "Text from Mom."

I take it warily.

Did you make the beds first thing?

My mother is very opinionated about moving.

Not yet, Mom.

Go do it before you and Jonah get tired. Trust me.

I roll my eyes at Brooks, who rolls his back, and head upstairs to take my mother's probably very sage advice. She has been more motherly toward me in the two years since Lucy's death, having laid off somewhat during Lucy's reign as queen of the household. Most of the time I appreciate it, because most of the time she's right, but it can also make me feel like I'm ten years old.

The box with the sheets also contains the contents of my nightstand drawers and all the stuff I swept off the surface during my rushed packing job. Once the two beds are made, I shove as much of the other crap as will fit into the drawers, then stack the rest on the surface of the nightstand. I don't do a very good job, though, and the whole thing rushes to the floor in a landslide—Clive Cussler, John le Carré, Lee Child, a few self-help books well-meaning people have tortured me with, and the spiral notebook where I keep my Lucy journal. The Lucy journal—basically, a daily letter to Lucy since her death—was the brainchild of the counselor at my grief group. *It won't bring them back,* she cautioned. *But it will help with the pain.*

I scoffed at the idea. I might even have made a scornful noise out loud. Anyone who knows me knows I'm not a journal guy, not a feelings guy, not a pour-it-all-out guy. But the idea must have stuck somewhere in the back of my mind, and one particularly bad night, I tried it. And, well, it kind of worked. It wasn't like she was right there in the room, but "talking" to her in the journal was a lot better than not talking to her at all.

I eye the journal guiltily. In the last couple of months, I've started a whole bunch of entries I haven't finished. *Tonight,* I promise myself. I restack the books, unfortunately just as precariously, with the journal on top as a reminder.

"Yo!" Brooks calls up the stairs. "Will you get down here and help me with this behemoth?"

He almost certainly means my kitchen table, which I built. The kitchen table is a heavy piece, made with reclaimed beams from old barns, fitted together to form a mosaic pattern. I'm pretty damn proud of it.

Brooks and I are carrying said table into the house when a voice calls to me from the next yard over. "Hey you! Young man!"

I look up to see my new next-door neighbor on the right side, a prune-faced white-haired lady standing on her front stoop, holding a jar.

"Which one of you is the new renter?"

We set down the table and I raise my hand, feeling like a kid who's about to get in trouble in school.

"That'd be me, ma'am. Sawyer. Sawyer Paulson."

"Well, Sawyer Paulson, when you get a chance, can you make yourself useful and come help me open this spaghetti sauce?"

"Happy to, ma'am." I cross my yard and unscrew the top of the marinara bottle.

"I'm Doris Wheeling," she says, accepting the open jar and lid back. "I'll try not to harass you, but even with that jar-opening thingie my son-in-law bought for me, I couldn't get this open."

"Happy to help anytime, ma'am." I scrounge in my pocket and find one of my furniture-making cards, frayed but serviceable. "Call or text my cell if you need jars opened."

She points behind me. "I think your son has found a friend."

Sure enough, when I turn around, Jonah is kneeling in the bushes beside another boy his age, inspecting something that from a distance looks like a small frog or a big bug.

"That's Elle's boy. Madden. They're your neighbors on the other side. It's just the two of them. You might offer to help her with her jars, too."

Did Doris Wheeling just make that sound really, really dirty?

"I um, I could do that." I cast a quick glance toward the house on the other side of mine. It's the twin to the one Jonah and I are renting, but infinitely better maintained.

Mrs. Wheeling taps arthritic fingers on the side of the jar, tugging my attention back to the conversation. "Anyway, thanks, Sawyer."

I nod. "Anytime."

"And a pleasure to meet you."

"Same here."

She gives me a lopsided smile, turns, and shuffles into her house.

I cast one more glance toward my other neighbor's house. *Elle*. Huh. Weird. I guess it's a more common name than I'd guessed.

Unless—

The thought is accompanied by a mental picture of soft

blond hair, perfect creamy breasts, and a plump lower lip slack with pleasure.

Nah. Wishful thinking.

I banish the sexy screen grab from my head and walk back to where Brooks is fidgeting with his phone. On his count of three, we hoist the table aloft and carry it inside.

"Couldn't you build this shit lighter?" Brooks groans.

I don't bother to answer him, just adjust my grasp to put more of the weight on him.

"You suck."

I lighten my own load a fraction more and smirk at him. "Remember, we share fifty percent genetic material."

I'm pleased that the table is so heavy he can't free a hand to flip me off.

2

ELLE

Hattie turns the wedding invitation over in her hands, eyeing it with loathing. "Do you want to burn it?"

I bite my lip. "I do, kind of, but I'm afraid I'll regret it later, when I come to my senses and realize I have to RSVP."

She raises her eyebrows. "You're not seriously thinking about going."

"Everything I've ever read online says I should go." I adopt an instructive tone. "'It's important to have an amiable relationship with your ex and his new wife, since they will be two of the most important people in your child's life.' Plus, if I don't go, don't I look like a total loser?"

I can tell from Hattie's expression that I'm about to get an earful. "You're seriously asking me that? He lied to you. He cheated on you. He left you. He only let eight weeks pass between your divorce becoming final and sending you a *wedding invitation,* and you're asking me if you look like a loser if you don't go to the wedding? Hell no, you'd be a spokesmodel for every woman in her right mind. 'Fuck that,

Big Asshole, no fucking way I'm going to your wedding.' Unless—"

She tucks her long, dark hair behind her ears and looks thoughtful. "Unless you can go with a really hot date. Then it might be worth it."

I scoff. "Sure. I'll just pull one of those out of my back pocket."

"Let's think. I've gotta know someone . . ."

Hattie, in fact, knows everyone, but the truth of the matter is that we live in the 'burbs, where single men are few and far between.

She sets the invitation back on the coffee table and I push it as far away from me as I can. When I saw it in my stack of mail, it only took me a split second to recognize what it was. My hands and feet went ice cold and I couldn't breathe. Then I opened it and saw their names side by side, gold text on ivory card stock, below a gold-leaf bride and groom. I almost threw up.

Thank God Madden was occupied playing with the new kid next door. I stumbled back to the house and called Hattie, who was over here ten minutes later with a bar of dark chocolate and a bottle of red wine.

Since Trevor left, Hattie's been my rock—she and our friend Capria, who couldn't be here today because she's at some kind of select soccer playoff thing with her oldest daughter. Hattie and Capria are both divorced, too.

I'm ashamed to admit now that before my life imploded, I didn't give other people's divorces much thought. It wasn't like when someone's spouse dies and everyone brings food and writes sympathy cards. I don't think I would have admitted this aloud, but I think I secretly believed divorce was a faux pas you should try not to draw attention to. Now that I'm on the other side of that equation, having gone through my own divorce, I know better. My personal opinion? People should bring you food and flowers. You need your friends more than ever when your marriage falls apart.

When Hattie and Capria heard that Trevor and I had split, they brought meals and wine and chocolate and lots of hugs. The first thing Hattie asked when she showed up at my door was, "Are we celebrating or mourning or a little of both?"

"D, none of the above: righteously pissed and nursing wounded pride," I told her, and she laughed and hugged me again, and said, "I remember that phase, too."

I'd had no idea that divorce came with such a wide spectrum of emotions, everything from crushing grief to raging anger.

These days, the big emotions are still lurking in the background, but I'm starting to want my old self back. Fearless, bright, happy Elle, the one who took contentment for granted. I see signs of her, peeking in around the edges, and I want to issue an invitation.

Part of me thinks if I can be a big enough girl to go to Trevor's wedding—to be his partner in parenting and as much of a friend as two exes can be—maybe I'll find that woman again.

Hattie has drifted toward the window. "I hope your new neighbor fixes that place up. It's such a dump. Oh, cute. Madden and the other boy are playing some game with a football and a Wiffle ball bat, and Madden is laughing."

"Score."

Madden's been having a tough time since the separation.

He misses seeing his dad on a daily basis. Sometimes he's angry—snapping at me for no reason or being sullen—and sometimes he's sad, moping around, unable to settle into any activity. I do everything I can—board games, movies, outings —but some days are just bad. I've been hopeful that having a new neighborhood friend his age might help bring him out of it. Cheering up Madden is part of my campaign to reclaim my life, too.

"It's supposed to be a single dad, right? Single dad and kid?"

"Yeah, that's what I heard. Haven't seen the dad yet, though." I head toward the window to peek out at Madden.

"Oh. Oh, *my*." Hattie's voice swoops.

"What?" I nudge her over to make room.

"You need a hot wedding date, right?"

Two very hot guys are moving furniture into the house next door. One is tall and broad-shouldered, with a full beard and mustache—very mountain man. The other is boy-next-door handsome, with rumpled light-brown hair and one of those perfectly proportioned male bodies—not too tall, not too short, not too muscly, not too skinny.

"Well, hello. You think one of those guys is my new neighbor?"

"There was another one, too. You just missed him. Tall and dark. Your type." She leers at me.

"Shut up."

She's still staring out the window. "You ever think about calling that guy?"

She's referring to the totally-out-of-character rebound sex I had right after the divorce papers were signed. I picked him up in a bar, which is so not my thing, but my friends had convinced me it was time to get back on the horse, and they were right. The guy I hooked up with was tall, dark, and broody, as unlike my ex-husband, Trevor, as it's possible to be, which may have been why I said yes when he offered to buy me a drink. And why I kept saying yes.

"He made it very clear he doesn't go back for seconds. And besides, I was such a dork that night, there's no way I could face him again."

"Too bad." Hattie knows: the sex was amazing.

I frown. "It was just the circumstances. The things that made him hot as a bar pickup wouldn't translate to real life. He'd probably turn out to be a jerk."

"They always do."

"Amen to that, sister."

Moment of silence for ex-husbands . . .

Hattie snaps her fingers. "I have a brilliant idea. Let's bake cookies and you can take them over tonight. Then you can meet your new neighbor . . . and *wedding date*."

I have to admit, it would be nice to have a date to Trevor's wedding. My showing up with a hot date wouldn't even ripple Trevor's pond, but showing up by myself—or chickening out completely—would just feel wrong. And even if Trevor doesn't give a crap what I do with my sex life, I want him to at least confront the fact that I still have one.

Sort of. Aside from that one act of rebound sex, it's been a barren year. But the rebound sex did make me determined to get back in the saddle. It reminded me that sex is too good to give up, even if I do plan to quit counting on men for anything other than orgasms.

"Anyway, regardless, we should make your new neighbors

cookies. I mean, what's the alternative? You want to sit here and stare at that invitation?"

"Hell no." The less time I spend thinking about Trevor's wedding, the better.

"So? Let's bake." Hattie drops the curtain.

We're elbow deep in cookie dough when I hear the back door open with enough force to smack it into the opposite wall. I sigh. Madden. I've asked him a million times, but he's not the best at being careful with stuff. I've mostly learned to take it in stride.

"Mom! Mom! This is Jonah! He's moving in next door!"

The two boys, muddy from the knees down, explode into the kitchen. Jonah's got longish dark hair that hangs in his face and brilliant blue eyes and looks vaguely familiar, like I know him from Madden's school. Eve—my Realtor friend—didn't know where they were moving from, so it might be somewhere in town.

"Mom, can Jonah sleep over here tonight? He likes to play Battlefront and baseball and football and I'm going to teach him how to play my Jukem and Minecraft card games. And can we watch *Cars 3* and will you make us popcorn?"

That might be the longest and most enthusiastic speech that Madden has made since Trevor moved out, and there's no way I'm saying no.

"Sure, if it's okay with his dad. Hi, Jonah. It's really nice to meet you. Welcome to the neighborhood. I'm Madden's mom. You can call me Elle, as long as your dad is okay with you using first names with grownups. And this is my friend Ms. Rivers."

"Hi," says Jonah politely. "It's nice to meet you."

"Come on come on come on, let's go play Jukem," says

Madden, and he and Jonah exit the kitchen in a flurry. I call after them, "Shoes off!" but it's probably too late. That's okay; I need to vacuum anyway.

"That was so stinkin' cute," Hattie says. "How crazy is it, how fast they make friends? A sleepover, and they've just met."

She smirks at me, and I throw a wad of paper towel at her.

3

ELLE

After Hattie leaves, Jonah and Madden are playing peacefully in Jonah's new front yard, so I pack up a foil-covered plate of cookies and carry it over to Mrs. Wheeling's house. Mrs. Wheeling is eighty-nine years old and has more energy than I do. When I show up with the cookies, she is making a lasagna for the family of a friend who recently died.

"Our new neighbor opened the jar of sauce for me," she informs me. "I didn't really need the jar opened, but I was trying to take his measure. He seems like a nice man. And it won't be the worst thing in the world to have a man with biceps like that mowing his lawn out there."

That's Mrs. Wheeling for you.

"Which one is the new neighbor? There were three guys out there earlier." I try very hard not to sound too interested, because Mrs. Wheeling will for sure pick up on it if I do. She was very kind to me for about a week after Trevor left, but ever since then, she's been doing more to try to get me laid than either Hattie or Capria. I was totally unsurprised, the first time I was in her bedroom, helping her reach something on a high-up closet shelf, to discover that her two small bookshelves are filled with romance novels. And not the ones with white picket fences and beaches on the cover, either. The kind with heroes with bare torsos and swim trunks hanging so low they reveal glistening hip-dip.

"The Heathcliff one," Mrs. Wheeling says, and my traitorous stomach swoops. I do so appreciate the merits of tall, dark, handsome, and broody. I have no intention of indulging myself in neighbor sex—too messy—but Mrs. Wheeling might have a point about the value of good-looking men on display in the yard. "Are you bringing him cookies, too?"

I nod.

"An excellent opening move."

"It's not a move," I say. "It's a gesture of neighborly warmth."

She narrows her eyes at me. "You believe whatever you want to believe. Have you seen his biceps?"

"I haven't," I admit.

"You have a treat in store."

"*You* could bring him cookies," I tease.

"They'd call me a cougar," she says, beaming with delight.

I ask after Mrs. Wheeling's son in eastern Washington and daughter on the East Coast, and her grandchildren (who are too far away), and then I say goodbye.

"Have fun *delivering cookies.*"

I love Mrs. Wheeling.

When I reach the new neighbors' yard, Jonah and Madden latch on to me like I'm the Pied Piper, even though they already had two cookies each at my house. They know that in all likelihood they'll be able to sucker Jonah's dad into giving them two more.

Even though I have Jonah with me, I knock on the front door. The Penske truck is gone—returned, I assume—and there's a pickup parked out front, a Ford F-150 four-door. Trevor used to say he was going to buy a Ford F-150—the two-door model—for his midlife crisis car. Too bad he didn't buy one instead of sleeping with his ex-girlfriend.

One of these days, I won't feel sick to my stomach when I think about Trevor's betrayal. But today is not that day.

I think it hurts so much partly because it wasn't just "someone else." It was a very specific someone else, the someone else I'd always been afraid he really loved. It was as if I'd convinced myself the unpleasant events around me were only a bad dream, then realized I was awake after all.

But that was then, and I'm doing everything I can to get past it.

I catch my breath, square my shoulders, and shake it off.

Jonah opens the door and yells over his shoulder, "Dad!"

I can see a narrow wedge of the house, including the staircase, so my first view of my new neighbor is of his bare feet as he descends. Then the hems of his jeans. Then his thighs. Okay, yeah. Mmm. And then—

Even though I really don't think you can tell that much about what a guy is packing under his jeans—because of the whole bluffer thing—I *am* staring. And maybe he's bluffing, but . . .

That's why it takes me a beat too long to meet his eyes (embarrassing), which is why I hear his intake of breath just a split second before I see his face.

Oh, *shit.*

My face goes flaming hot, and I'm not sure if it's from shame or lust.

The guy standing in the doorway is Tall, Dark, and Broody. *The* Original Tall, Dark, and Broody, as in my rebound sex guy.

Dark eyes. Dark hair. Strong jaw, shadowed with late-day stubble. A body so built he fills my field of vision, a broad chest swelling under a soft cotton T, and those spectacular biceps, which deserve every ounce of Mrs. Wheeling's praise.

The next set of images are memories, a wash of sensation as vivid as a dream in progress: him looming over me just before his mouth seals mine in a kiss, his body crowding mine against the brick wall of the alley outside the bar, the heat and size and thickness of him like a drug I can't get enough of. His mouth, tasting of scotch, and his tongue, soft as velvet, stroking all my tender corners so by the end of the first kiss I am already thinking of all the places I want his touch. His callused hand pushing my skirt up, finding and tearing my underpants, his fingers sliding headlong through my slickness, the one he slipped into my core thick enough for me to clench around, but his thumb on my clit still nimble enough to bring me off in the space of ten heartbeats.

It's possible I make a sound, nowhere near audible enough to be a moan or a whimper, more like a huff of surprise.

"Dad! Dad!" Jonah says. "Can I have a sleepover at Madden's house?"

Tall, Dark, and Broody's eyes haven't left my face.

"Well," he says. "We meet again."

4

SAWYER

When Lucy was alive, shit like this just didn't happen.

The last time I saw this woman, she was leaning against a brick wall with her skirt hiked up and her eyes closed, trying to catch her breath. A few minutes after that, I was in my car, driving away, feeling the mix of relief and remorse that has accompanied every encounter I've had since Lucy's death. Also, feeling like an asshole for more or less running away after sex.

Now I'm standing in the doorway of the new rental, and she's flanked by her son and mine, who are apparently, inconveniently, already best buds. She's holding a foil-wrapped plate in her hands, which she thrusts out. "I made you some cookies. I mean, because you're the new neighbors, not because you and I—"

She stops, obviously realizing that there is nowhere good that sentence can go.

When I spotted her across the room at Maeve's, she was the prettiest girl in a room of pretty girls. She's still that pretty.

She's small (*which made it easy to lift her up against the wall and —*), maybe five foot four, with California-girl shiny, straight blond hair, and a heart-shaped face with blue eyes and a beautiful wide mouth (*which feels even better than it looks; her lips really* are *that soft and she does this thing with her tongue, urging mine on*), which is painted with pale-pink lipstick (*but that night was bright, glossy fuck-me-dead red*). And she looks really uncertain today, which I would think was because of the awkward situation except she looked that way that night too (*except when I was inside her, cupping her head to keep her from banging it against the alley wall, when her face was all unlocked, bold pleasure*).

She is so not supposed to be on my doorstep. She was supposed to be a one-night-only fling.

She takes a deep breath and starts over. "Welcome to the neighborhood. I'm Elle Dunning."

I raise my eyebrows. She told me her first name the night we met, and I haven't forgotten. But I guess we're going to pretend that whole thing didn't happen. Which is good. The last thing I want is to have stranger-fucked my new neighbor. And enjoyed it. A lot.

Jesus.

"Sawyer. Paulson." I take the plate of cookies she's still offering me. "Thanks."

I suck at words. Just—I suck. I have a lot of them in my head, but they never come out when I need them. It's ten times worse with women, too.

"Madden and I are very happy to have you and Jonah here and we just wanted to let you know that if you need anything, we're right next door."

She is perky in that plastic, faux-chipper way that women

put on when they're trying to make a good impression, and I realize that if this were the first time I was meeting her, I would think she was wound way too tight.

I know from personal experience she's not uptight. Anything but, at least not when it comes to sex. She's willing, responsive . . .

Speaking of tight, my jeans are feeling a little uncomfortable.

"Madden invited Jonah to sleep over and I said it was fine with me if it's fine with you. The boys seem to be getting along great. Which is terrific! I'm super glad! We're very happy to have another boy Madden's age in the neighborhood."

"Dad, can I? Can I?"

"I—"

"Please?"

"I guess so." I'm busy trying to think what Lucy would do in this situation—invite them in? Exchange phone numbers? Would she let Jonah sleep at a house of people he'd just met? Where the hell is the sleeping bag? Jonah's pillow? His *pajamas*?

Of course Lucy wouldn't be in this situation, ever, and neither would I, if Lucy were still here.

"Jonah can borrow some of Madden's stuff," Elle says brightly. "We have lots of things; he'll be just fine."

She's breathlessly cheerful. The night we fucked, she was like this, too, filling all the space between us with words. She would have talked more, except eventually I stopped the words with my mouth. I can't do that now.

Though it's tempting.

And an unbelievably shitty idea.

"So, um—yeah! Anyway, we're right over here if you need anything, and, um, let me give you my cell number so you can text if you need Jonah back in the morning." She takes her phone out and I have a vivid flashback to that night, when she grabbed my phone out of my hand, snapped my photo, and texted it to her friend so that—her words—if I left her body in a ditch, the police artist's job would be easier.

It had made me laugh, a laugh I could feel in my chest but that hadn't quite made it to the surface. Laughter, like words, often got stuck partway out, since Luce's death.

Now I take my phone out and we exchange numbers—I punch mine into her phone and then she texts me.

"Got it. Thanks."

There's an awkward silence.

"Right," she says brightly. "So, um, really nice to meet you. Glad to have you in the neighborhood, and all that. See you around."

And she's gone, the boys trailing her, already plotting something to do with popcorn and a movie, and I stare after her, realizing I said maybe four words to her the whole time.

"'Bye," I say, to the empty air.

5

ELLE

I t's him.

And—once again, I babbled like my mouth was on autopilot and my brain was disengaged.

It's something about him. It's because he doesn't talk. He's just this big, silent presence, and I feel like I have to provide all the words to fill the empty space.

I can't believe the one stranger I've had sex with in my entire life is now living next door to me.

How does stuff like this even happen?

I get the boys set up with their movie, and then I sit down at the kitchen table with a *big* glass of wine and text Hattie. *You are not going to believe this. It's him. The rebound guy. Living next door. What do I do?*

OMG are you serious?

Dead serious.

Long silence.

Fuck him again? 😬

I laugh. Because that's so Hattie.

No way! Our kids are friends! He said it was a one-time thing!

I babbled my whole angsty story in one big drunken word-vomit! I could barely look him in the eye today!

Okay. Don't panic. Did he say anything about it?

Just "Well, we meet again." And then we pretty much pretended it never happened.

That doesn't sound so bad. Do you think you can pretend it never happened?

Do I have a choice?

Long silence.

No, probably not. Do you want me to come over?

No, I'm OK. I'll be OK. It's probably not really such a big deal. I just wish I'd known before I let Madden fall in friend-love with his son.

You wouldn't have been able to keep them apart anyway. Two eight year old boys living next door? Fat chance.

They're having a sleepover.

Awkward! But you can probably mostly avoid him. Communicate by text and by boy-message.

Yeah.

Text if you need me.

I set my phone down and lean my head in my hands.

It makes me mad at Trevor all over again, because if he hadn't broken my heart, I wouldn't have been looking for action in a bar, and if I hadn't been looking for action in a bar, I wouldn't have slept with Sawyer, and if I hadn't slept with Sawyer, I wouldn't be living next door to a guy I can picture in the throes of pleasure, his head tipped back and the cords in his neck straining—

White-hot need flares in my stomach.

Shit!

It happened two months ago, the Saturday night after the divorce was finalized. Hattie insisted it was time for me to get my groove back on—and I couldn't argue, because I was ready to find my old, fun self. I'd loved Trevor so much and I'd been wrecked by the betrayal, but I wasn't going to let him ruin my life permanently, either. So I parked Madden with my mom for an overnight.

Hattie said we needed to go to Maeve's, a bar a couple of towns over that was the best place she knew to meet someone for a hookup—but not (she promised) in a sleazy way. It was a huge bonus that Maeve's wasn't right in Revere Lake, because Revere Lake is a small town and everyone knows everyone else's business. You don't want to hook up with someone and then discover that he's your kid's second-grade teacher or your new gyno.

(Or your next-door neighbor. But apparently hooking up a few towns over isn't proof against that.) I cringe.

Anyway, Hattie, Capria, Hattie's friend Juno, and I went out together.

Maeve's is an old roadhouse—wood walls, posts and beams, big tables and lots of booths, plastic menus. I think some of the street signs and posters and photos and maps on the walls probably date back to saloon days. It just got bought by new owners a couple of months ago—word is, they're committed to keeping the feel the same—and the night we were there, you could hear occasional hammering from behind the back wall of the bar, where some unlucky construction overtimers were working on an addition for more seating and a stage for concerts.

The four of us ordered dinner and drinks and sat around, chatting and laughing and flirting with whoever looked our way. Unfortunately, Hattie came down with the stomach flu about an hour into the night and Juno drove her home.

Capria and I hung around for a while longer. We chatted with guys who approached our table, but none of them spun my dials and I wasn't really sure what I'd do if one did, anyway. The drunker I got, the more I wanted to go home to sleep.

After a while, Capria took pity on me. "You want to head out?"

If Hattie had still been there, she would never have let me off the hook, even if it meant personally marching up to some guy and telling him I was looking for a one-night rebound fling. But Capria is a lot softer.

I nodded.

"Okay. I'm just going to hit the ladies' and we'll go."

She'd been gone less than a minute when I noticed the guy staring in my direction from his seat at the bar. Incredibly good-looking, in a football-player-meets-male-model way—tall, built, with near-black hair, dark eyes, and a couple of days' scruff on his jaw. He wasn't smiling. Of course, I looked behind me to see if he was scoping out someone else. That's how badly Trevor had messed with my self-confidence.

When I looked back in his direction, the guy shook his head. *You,* he mouthed, and the invitation in his eyes and on his lips was unmistakable.

A wave of warmth poured over me, like someone had doused me with heated honey. All the numbness lifted off. Everything came back to life—with a vengeance.

Oh, hello, girl parts. You are *still down there.*

He raised his glass and cocked his head, a clear, *Can I buy you a drink?*

I froze like a deer in the headlights.

Suddenly Capria was standing in my line of sight, which felt like a reprieve. I could pretend I hadn't seen the guy offer to buy me a drink, I could get a ride home from Capria, and I could go back to—

Being numb.

No way! cried my girl parts.

"Elle?" Capria peered curiously at me.

That was when I started to think about how much Trevor would hate this guy on sight, and for no legit reason. Trevor has a skinny nerd's built-in envy of alpha males. They make him twitchy, juvenile, and competitive, like he never got the seventh-grader out of him.

I immediately wanted to have sex with the guy at the bar on principle. Not, like I said, that Trevor actually gives a shit what I do. But I thought he'd loathe the idea of me fucking this guy anyway.

"I know I said I wanted to head out, but would you hate me if I had a drink with the guy at the bar who just offered to buy me one? Don'tlooknow!" I added hastily.

She slid into her seat, checking him out. "Woo, girl! No! I would hate you if you didn't. *And* I want to hear all about it after. Mmm-*hmm.*" She shook her head. "Next time *you're* going to the bathroom and I'm taking home the prize."

I caught his eye across the room and mouthed, *Sure,* with a little nod. His gaze heated in approval, nudging another chain reaction to life under my skin.

How did anyone manage to look so much like sex on a stick? The way he was staring at me, I could imagine the expression he'd wear when I went down on him, full of abandon and gratitude.

Had I really just thought about going down on a guy I hadn't even introduced myself to yet?

Mmm-hmm, said the Greek chorus below.

"Go. Get." Capria shooed me.

"You can go. Take your car. I'll Uber." That suddenly made it real, what I was about to do. "I've never done this," I confessed. "Gone home with a guy I met in a bar."

Capria grinned. "You're like a hookup virgin! Ask him for his phone, take a picture of him, and send a text to me so I have his phone number and photo."

"That's not going to keep him from killing me and tossing my body in a Dumpster."

"No, but it will probably keep him from killing the girl after you," Capria said with a wry grin.

I made a face at her. "Thanks. Helpful."

I slid out of my seat, then paused. On one side of the divide was safe and numb, and on the other side—

Let's go! my body crowed.

I left Capria, crossed the crowded, noisy room, and slid onto the stool next to his. Up close, I could feel the heat of his body, and something else, a humming current of attraction. He smelled like soap and just the right amount of some spicy cologne. I wanted to lean in and breathe him deep.

"What do you drink?" No hello. He didn't even turn his body toward the stool where I sat. Which was okay, because he had a terrific profile.

"Peach on the beach," I told the bartender. I extended my hand. "I'm Elle."

He turned and took my hand in his. His was big, his palm callused, his skin warm. "Sawyer."

"Are you from around here?"

"Couple towns east. Geneva." His speech was rough and short. I wanted to run a thumb over it, the way I wanted to reach out and feel the shadow of dark stubble on his jaw.

"I'm from the other direction, a couple towns west," I said, smiling, noting how unafraid guys are to give out personal information, and how cautious I felt about telling him where I lived, even though I was planning, potentially, on having sex with him. "My friends said Maeve's was the place to be."

"It really is," he said, looking around. Eighties music blared from the speakers and a throng had formed on the dance floor. People were kissing and grinding and groping. Sex was everywhere. I could feel it wriggling in my bloodstream, too.

Capria waved at us from the edge of the horde.

"That's my friend Capria."

He waved back. She gave him the two-fingered *I'm watching you* sign. He held up his whiskey in a toast and drank.

"She's got your back," he observed. "So what brings you guys to Maeve's tonight?"

"This was my friends' idea. My divorce just got finalized. Shit," I said, biting my lip. "I wasn't going to say that. I wasn't going to talk about my divorce at all."

Hattie had coached me. Keep it light . . .

He shrugged. "It's okay. Divorced is good. Better, in this case, than married."

That made me smile. "Depends on your perspective, I guess."

"Not so good from your perspective?"

"It's been a shitty year."

My drink came and I drank it too fast. He raised his eyebrows. "You want to tell me about your shitty year?"

"Um, you don't really want to hear it."

"You should let me be the judge of that."

"It's in the rules book. Don't talk about your divorce when you're trying to hook up with a guy in a bar."

I clamped my mouth shut. My face was bright red. I almost jumped off my stool and fled. I'd just voiced a mammoth assumption.

"Hookup, huh?" The hint of a smile tipped up the corner of his mouth.

"Shit," I said. "You know what? Maybe I'd better leave before I totally humiliate myself."

"No. Don't do that. It's a hookup. If you want it to be." His gaze swept over me, bringing heat everywhere it touched. "*I* do."

His frankness flooded me with relief. My nerves notched down.

"Yeah. My friends think it's time to get back on the hor—"

I cut myself off, blushing furiously.

Damn alcohol. Next thing you know, I'd be telling him the sordid details of exactly how Trevor had hurt me.

"Well, lucky me for being in the right place at the right time." He watched me intently. I was drunk enough now that I was starting to get that tunnel effect—I could feel the music throbbing, the ruckus of the voices around me, but mostly I could see him—those heavy-lidded dark eyes, his full mouth, the knot of muscle at his jaw.

I could feel the seam of my jeans against the seam of my sex, my clit swollen there. I was usually slow to heat up. This was some crazy intense chemistry. Or too much alcohol.

"I think you should tell me about your shitty year." He raised his eyebrows. "Unless you'd rather make small talk."

I smiled at that. "Um, not particularly."

He had this patient way of listening. He was very still, and he looked right into my eyes.

I figured, what the hell? I didn't need him to like me. I just needed him to sleep with me. "He left me for his high school girlfriend."

He winced.

"Yeah. He was still dating her in college, long distance, right before I met him. I was his rebound from her, except then I got pregnant and we got married. But somewhere in there, he decided that she really was the one. They kept in touch the whole time, and I had no idea how much he messaged and texted her. Skyped her, even. He said it only ever crossed the line into being physical once, like it was supposed to make me feel better that he only emotionally cheated on me, or like I'm supposed to congratulate him on his restraint. I couldn't stop thinking about that one time, though—trying to figure out what it was, when it happened —Shit," I said again, "I'll shut up now. Has anyone ever told you you're easy to talk to?"

"Not really." This time I was sure of it: that slight quirk at the corner of his mouth was a hint of a smile.

"I babble when I'm nervous."

"Why are you nervous?"

He didn't ask it in a mean way. He asked like he really wanted to know.

"I've never done this. I mean, I had high school and college hookups at parties and stuff, but that was different. I was married when I was twenty-two. I had a kid when I was twenty-three. So this is my first bar hookup."

My face flamed. *Way to go, Elle. Now he's* really *turned on.*

He finished his whiskey, and I was half expecting him to make some excuse and walk away, but instead he reached his hand out and brushed his thumb across my lower lip. "You have a beautiful mouth."

Heat washed through me, and I drew a shuddering breath.

His eyes darkened. "Yeah? You like that? What do you need?"

I wasn't sure I knew the answer.

He read my confusion.

"You need to fuck? Prove you can still do it? That your ex didn't take it away from you?"

Unable to speak, I nodded. The casual way he said "fuck" had slipped under all my defenses and burrowed itself into the hot, wet center of me. And it felt good to admit the truth.

His mouth quirked in an almost-smile. "Works for me. As long as you know this is a one-time thing, though. I don't do repeats, no matter what."

I didn't want a repeat. Sawyer was exactly right. I wanted to prove to myself (and Trevor, even if he wasn't actually ever going to know) that Trevor hadn't broken me.

And I wanted to prove it with this guy, who was still looking at me like he wanted to spread me out on the bar and do wonderful terrible things to me.

I was pretty sure no one had ever looked at me like that before.

My throat was so tight with desire and anticipation that I couldn't speak.

His hand came up again, cupped my cheek and slid around the back of my head, fingers thrusting into my hair. He leaned down and kissed me. His mouth was warm and his tongue licked peach off mine. I moaned.

He threw a couple of twenties on the bar and pulled me off my stool.

I remembered Capria's safety advice. "Give me your phone."

He handed it over without question. He'd done this before. A hundred times, for all I knew.

I snapped his photo, texted it to Capria. "So if they find my body in a ditch the police artist has something to work with."

I couldn't read the expression on his face, but he bent to kiss me again, so fiercely I lost my breath.

We made it only as far as the alley before he had me pressed between brick and his body.

6

SAWYER

I have the house to myself. Jonah is next door for the night. I start unpacking boxes, but I don't get very far. I keep having sex-with-Elle flashbacks. But the funny thing is, they aren't about the dirtiest part of what I did to her against the brick wall in an alleyway beside a bar. No, the thing I can't stop thinking about is how cute she was when she was drunk. I don't usually like women who blab—I hate gossip and small talk and the kind of nervous-polite chitchat Elle was making earlier today.

But that night, the way she kept blurting things out made me want to smile, and I hadn't wanted to smile about much in a long, long time.

The thing was, I didn't *want* to want to smile, if you know what I mean.

And I really didn't want a woman to be the thing making me want to smile.

Smiling at a cute woman made me think about Lucy, and that sucked. Because what Lucy and I had—it wasn't going to come around again.

Lucy was the only woman I'd ever loved, and I'm pretty sure she's the only woman I'll ever love.

For one thing, I'm not the kind of guy who falls in love. I guess maybe you could say I'm a misanthrope. Or maybe just a loner. Whatever. At any rate, there aren't very many people in the world I genuinely like spending time with. Brooks and Chase, in small doses. And Jonah—but I figure that's because in that respect he's kind of a mini-me—a loner, too.

And for a while there, there was Lucy.

Lucy was the one woman I ever knew who didn't seem to think there was something wrong with me, who wasn't always trying to offer me a penny for my thoughts or get me to talk more. And the funny thing was, that made me more talkative. It was like during the time I was with Lucy, there was a light on inside me. And when she died—

Well, it went out.

And I don't know if I want it lit again. Because the snuffing out was pretty much the most awful, painful thing you can possibly imagine. Watching Lucy fade away, from who she was to, well, nothing . . .

Yeah. Not going there.

Anyway, the odds that there's someone else out there who could do that to me—light me up like that again?

Not playing that lottery.

Which is why anything that makes me think about Lucy and what we had is also incredibly painful.

So when Elle's goofy chatter thing made me like her just a little bit that night at Maeve's, I wanted to get back on solid ground. I was comfortable with sex. I'd had lots of it. At least once a week since a month or two after Lucy died—pickups, hookups, always an up-front "one-time-only" warning, as impersonal as jerking off.

No smiling. No enjoying myself. No liking anyone or finding her cute. (Hot, yes. Sexy, yes. Filthy, naughty, delicious —all okay.) Cute, no way. Because among other things, I knew I had nothing to give in a relationship. And I didn't want one.

Then Elle said the dorky thing about it being her first hookup and she blushed.

Cute.

I finished my whiskey, and instead of getting up like I knew I should, I followed an impulse that felt more dangerous than pretty much any of the impersonal sex I'd had since Luce died.

I touched her. Ran my thumb over her lower lip.

It was like touching a live wire. Not just because I felt the touch flick back over my own nerves, but because she reacted, quicksilver and perfect. Her lips parted on a silent gasp, and her pupils flared.

I wanted to make her do it again. I wanted to make her feel it again, whatever she'd just felt.

I wanted to know exactly what it was, too. I wanted her to tell me. I guess that's part of why I asked her that crazy question. *You need to fuck? Prove you can still do it? That your ex didn't take it away from you?*

I just knew, somehow. I knew that was how she felt. Like he'd taken away something that belonged to her. And I also knew I could give it back to her.

When I said the word *fuck,* her pupils flared again. She liked it; she was dirty to the core. But also scared and vulnerable and—

I'm hard.

Now, I mean. Standing in my new kitchen, a coffee mug in one hand and a bunch of newspaper in the other hand, in an Elle trance. My dick is pumped full of blood, just like it was that night when I took her hand and led her outside and lifted her up so I could brace her against the wall. I have no idea how I had the wherewithal to slow things down enough to bring her off before I plowed into her, but somehow I managed it. Rucked her skirt up, ripped her panties trying to get them out of my way, slid one finger into her wet heat, slicked the swollen nub of her clit until she came clenching around my touch. So fucking hot I almost spilled in my briefs, which would have been an embarrassing (and unprecedented) end to a potential hookup.

My hand is in my jeans. In my briefs. Straightening myself out.

I slowly become aware that I am in a lit room with no curtains and it is growing dark outside. I have enough living brain cells not concentrated in my dick to get myself around the corner into the area behind the stairs so I'm not visible from the street or either of my neighbors' houses. But that's as far as I get before I unzip my jeans, free my erection from my briefs, and wrap my fist tight around myself.

That night, I got the condom on so fast that she was still coming when I filled her. Clenching around me, fluttering, whimpering, clutching my arms, my hair, anything she could get her hands on. She gasped at every thrust, pressing herself down on me like she couldn't get enough.

It was the best kind of sex, the kind you want to go on for hours that has no prayer of lasting more than seconds.

I came so fast, so hard, that I figured I owed her a big apology, except when I started to regain some semblance of conscious thought I realized she was coming again, clamping down around me, biting the crap out of my arm to keep from making noise.

I yell something incoherent and christen my new house with an epic fountain of cum, coating my hands and dousing my shirt.

Laundry. Damn. Gotta install the washer and dryer.

Rookie.

7

ELLE

I'm making pancakes for the boys when the doorbell rings.

"Madden! Can you get that?"

There's no answer. Madden and Jonah are downstairs playing in a fort they built, and I'm guessing with the basement door closed and the blankets and pillows muffling their ears, they can't hear me. Or their hearing has grown selective because they're immersed in their own imaginative world . . .

I head for the door myself.

It's Sawyer.

I'm startled, anew, by just how big he is, and how attractive. He's wearing a pair of camel-colored Carhartts and a black T-shirt that says *Emily's,* with a cartoon picture of a fifties club-car diner. The T-shirt fits gorgeously over his broad shoulders and chest and I remember, with a rush of desire, how those muscles flexed under my hands. His hair is damp, as though he's fresh from the shower, and I can't help myself: I breathe deeply—but surreptitiously—and catch a whiff of Lever. Damn. I'm a sucker for that soap.

"Sorry." As usual, his delivery is gruff. It roughs up my nerve endings in a way I'd like to hate but can't. "I texted but you didn't answer, so I came over. I was hoping to take Jonah for a hike. I wanted to grab him in an hour or so."

"Sure, no problem. The boys are up. I was about to feed them some pancakes. I'm making them now."

"I figured." He gestures with a tilt of his head at my hand, which—I now realize—is clutching a spatula. "At least, that was my best guess." He raises an eyebrow.

Damn him. That eyebrow quirk ripples through all the earthquake-prone bits of me.

He, on the other hand, is unfazed. He shifts away from the door, indicating the conversation is over. "If you could just let Jonah know. Madden's welcome too."

"Welcome where?" Madden demands, materializing with Jonah in tow.

"On a hike with Mr. Paulson and Jonah."

"A long hike?"

I look to Sawyer.

"Couple miles. Not super long. Really great view at the end."

"Can I, Mom?"

Obviously, according to the workings of Murphy's Law, these two boys are going to be inseparable. But I'll just have to live with that, and find ways not to have to be face-to-face with Sawyer. I can be a big girl about it. "Um, Dad is taking you to his place for dinner tonight, so—would he be back by dinnertime? Before five?" I address these questions to Sawyer. Five is when Trevor is scheduled to pick Madden up.

"We should be back before that."

"Sure, you can go," I tell Madden, who bounces on his toes in jubilation.

"You should hike with us too," Jonah says to me.

"Um, thanks." I don't meet Sawyer's eyes. He makes no move to reinforce Jonah's invitation, so I figure he's as horrified by the thought as I am. "That's, um, super nice. But I've got a lot of things to do. Writing. I have a bunch of articles due. I have a freelance writing business—" I stop just in time, before I can fully gear up into babble territory.

"Mr. Paulson, you should come in and have some pancakes," Madden says. "My mom makes the best pancakes."

They really are such delightful, polite, kind boys, and yet I want to shake them right now. I mutter, "Yes, you should have some pancakes with us." It's the most ungracious invitation ever issued, and I imagine my mother, who is a stickler for manners, shaking her finger at me.

"Already ate," Sawyer says. "Thanks. So yeah. Send the boys my way."

And on that note, without an actual goodbye, he turns and heads back to his house.

I sigh and close the door, leaning against it like that might shut out some portion of either my unruly attraction or my embarrassment. Or just keep him from ever showing up on my doorstep again.

Except I liked having him on my doorstep. The problem is maybe that I liked it a little too much.

This is a one-time thing. I don't do repeats, no matter what.

Which is totally fine, right? I wouldn't want a repeat.

Right?

"Mom, what's that smell?" Madden asks, snapping me

back to the present, which features the distinctive odor of burning pancake.

"Shit!" I cry, running back into the kitchen in time to prevent a fire, but not to save the charred pancakes on the griddle.

As I'm scraping those pancakes into the trash and starting a new set, I realize that not only was I clutching a spatula throughout the entire conversation with Sawyer, I was also wearing my rubber-duck shorty pajamas and a gag apron that Trevor gave me for Christmas two years ago that says, *Ask me about my explosive diarrhea.*

I guess humiliation is going to be the name of this particular game.

8

SAWYER

"How was the sleepover?" I ask the boys over my shoulder as we drive out to my favorite kid-friendly trail, the overlook from Mount Mocadney.

"Fun!" Jonah says.

I catch a glimpse of my son's face in the rearview mirror. In place of his usual expression of pre-teenage boredom, he's grinning. I can't help smiling in response, although I know he can't see me.

"What'd you guys do?"

"Played Battlefront. Played Jukem. Watched *Cars 3*. Had a pillow fight."

"Ms. Dunning must have loved that."

In the rearview mirror, the boys exchange quick, knowing glances.

"My mom was a little mad. But not really mad," Madden informs me. "She laughed after."

I try to picture what Elle must look like in a parental lather, but my imagination fails me. My brain serves up another image instead. The night I met her, the way she looked right after I kissed her. Her mouth was kiss-slick, her lips parted, her eyes hazy with desire.

Okay, then.

Last night, while Jonah was at Madden's, I went out for beers with my brother and our friends. And I may or may not have mentioned the situation I've found myself in—next door to a one-night stand, whose kid is my kid's brand new bestie. If I'd been looking for sympathy, I was definitely out of luck. They thought it was the funniest thing they'd ever heard.

The beer was more sympathetic than they were.

I wrench my mind back to the present. Pillow fight. "Nothing got broken, did it?"

"Nah," Jonah says.

"So, Madden, your mom's a writer?" I tell myself I'm just making conversation with Jonah's new friend, that I'm not indulging my curiosity about the woman next door.

"Yup. She writes for magazines and stuff."

"Pretty cool. She written any books?"

"Not yet, but she says she wants to someday."

"Do you like to write?"

"Not really." I glimpse the tail end of Madden's shrug.

"So what do you and your mom do for fun?"

Madden appears to consider that at length. "We used to have more fun before my dad left," he says.

Ouch. Of all people, I should have known better than to poke that wound. I'm sure similar words could have come out of Jonah's mouth.

"I bet you still do fun stuff sometimes," I prompt, trying to undo the damage I've done by opening this topic.

Madden thinks, then brightens. "We go to movies and

play games. And Mom says we're going to kayak this summer and hike and stuff. She says this summer will be funner than last summer because things were kind of messed up last summer. 'Cause you know my dad went to go be with Helen, who was his high school girlfriend, and it really, really, really hurt my mom's feelings."

I feel a sharp pinch of sympathy for Elle. It's mingled with respect, too, because it sounds like she was pretty truthful with Madden, without flat-out making Trevor into the bad guy. That's not so easy to do.

"My feelings were hurt, too," Madden says, matter-of-factly.

"Yeah," I say. "Really, really hurt feelings would definitely make sense in that situation. But I bet you and your mom take good care of each other."

"We do!"

"And she seems like a pretty fun mom."

I flash on another image of Elle, at odds with the earlier one: her wearing rubber-duck pajamas and a diarrhea-joke apron, her hair up in a messy bun, clutching a spatula. I have to fight back a smile.

"She *is*," Madden says emphatically.

Shortly after that, the boys conk out in the backseat. They probably didn't sleep much, what with video games, movies, board games, and pillow fights.

The car takes on that soothing feeling I used to love when Lucy and Jonah both fell asleep on a drive, and I realize, with a start, that this will be the first time Jonah and I have hiked Mount Mocadney without Lucy. Lucy and I used to do this hike all the time with Jonah when he was little, making a day of it and packing lunches, snacks, and water bottles.

I can't believe it's been two years since I've been up here. I guess I took a break from being fun after Lucy's death, too.

When we used to do this trip as a family, Lucy and I fought, not angrily but in the way people do who love each other but are together all the time. I never understood why the whole trip had to be such a production, why she got so fussy about whether we were dressed right for the weather and had enough food to survive an apocalypse. If I suggested that it was more important to catch the best part of the day than to be equipped for disaster, she got mad at me for being so cavalier. But not really mad. Just, you know, pissy. The sandpapery rub of two people's neuroses against each other.

I miss it. The day-to-day reality, even the fighting.

I wonder if Jonah will remember that we used to do this with his mom. I wonder if he'll feel like it was more fun *before.*

I'm suddenly so glad I brought Madden along for distraction. It'll be different-fun with him.

I find a parking space, despite all the people who've had the same idea we did. The boys wake as the car stops and bound out, going from fast asleep to wide awake so fast it makes me crave coffee. They skip toward the wooden stand that holds the area map and study it, but I can tell as I get close that they don't really understand it. So I boost them up one at a time and let them get a closer look, show them the "You Are Here" sticker and where we're headed. Then I point them at the trailhead and let them run.

They dash ahead of me on the trail, Jonah with his jet-black mop and Madden, who's a dandelion, with fluffy butter-blond hair and skinny limbs. The fact that they're moving so fast is great, because it means that I have to walk at a pretty good clip to keep up with them. But it also means that they're lost in their own world, some mix of woods exploration and video game culture. I hurry after them, admiring the late spring woods, the ferns unfurling, the ground russet with needles. My mind drifts, from the sights around me to my plans for the house (first, get rid of the heinous carpet in the living room), and I let it wander wherever it wants to go.

Oddly enough, as I catch up to the boys near the overlook, I realize that I haven't mostly been thinking about Lucy.

Which is weird, because I must have walked this trail twenty or more times with her, wearing the backpack she'd crammed with supplies. While we walked, we chatted. Sometimes it was good, her sharing a funny story or something about her shop, or me talking about a piece of furniture I was working on. Sometimes it was bad, the two of us spatting over whether we had enough money to fix a broken oven or who was going to call around to find out who could do the repairs.

Today, though, those memories aren't the thoughts that mostly fill my head.

Instead, it's the sight of Elle dressed as she was earlier today, in those ridiculous shorty pajamas and that awful apron, spatula in hand.

I chuckle, thinking of it.

But barely suppressed laughter wasn't my only reaction.

Standing there on her front stoop, part of me wanted to complete my mission as soon as possible and escape to the safety of my house.

Another part of me wanted something else. The part of me that remembered.

How her hair felt like handfuls of silk.

How her nipples rose under my touch, hard and needy.

How soft the skin of her inner thighs felt, rich and delicate, begging to be licked.

I wanted it again.

I wanted to unfasten the messy bun and let all that blond goodness tumble down around her shoulders so I could run my fingers through it.

I wanted to untie her apron and let it drop to the floor, then brush her nipples to peaks through the thin cloth of her shorty pajamas, because I'd bet the farm she wasn't wearing a bra.

I wanted to take my time running my hands—and my tongue—up the satin expanse of leg revealed beneath the shorty bottoms.

But it wasn't the remembering or the physical craving that had me tied in knots.

No. It was how badly I'd wanted to knock on her door and tell her I'd changed my mind, that I'd happily accept her invitation to join her and the boys for pancakes.

How close I'd come to doing it.

9

ELLE

At 5:01, the doorbell rings.

Damn.

I was really, really, really hoping that Madden got home before Trevor showed up. Because the less conversation I have to make with Trevor, the better.

But about an hour ago, I got a message from Sawyer that said:

Running late. GPS says ETA 5:05.

No worries, I texted back. Trevor's usually a few minutes late anyway.

No such luck.

Trevor stands on the front steps. He's tall, almost six feet, built like a runner, with reddish-blond hair that tends toward wild and is too long right now. I used to love his hair too long. I would run my fingers through it, feeling the strands sift like sand.

Now I want to tell him to get it cut.

"Hi," he says.

"Hi. Come in."

If Madden were here, I would have pushed him out the door the instant Trevor's car pulled up at the curb, hoping to forestall this awkwardness. And I probably would have succeeded, because Trevor's no more eager to talk to me than I am to talk to him.

I can't live a lie anymore.

That's what he said to me. That he'd feel—every day for the rest of his life—that he was living a lie if he stayed with me instead of divorcing me and marrying Helen Bradley.

He felt horrible saying it. I could tell. Which didn't make it hurt even one iota less.

He steps into the foyer. His eyes dart around, looking for salvation.

"Madden should be here any minute. I let him go for a hike with the new neighbors, and they're a few minutes late getting back."

"New neighbors in the Snyders' house? You didn't tell me it was for rent again."

Yeah. About that. I didn't tell Trevor it was for rent because I didn't want him getting any insane ideas that maybe he and Helen should move in there.

Trevor lives in Seattle now, in the Broadview neighborhood, in his new fiancée's house. They have Madden every other weekend, half of Madden's school vacations, and every other week in the summer. Trevor wanted fifty-fifty custody, but he agreed with me that it wouldn't make sense unless he and Helen were living closer. Neither of us wanted Madden's school life disrupted.

Luckily for me on a number of counts, Trevor and Helen have not yet gotten their act together to buy a house closer to me.

I am grateful on a daily basis that Trevor and Helen don't live in Revere Lake. It would be so uncomfortable for me to have my ex and his lover in the house next door, to watch their comings and goings, to maybe even one summer night hear them—Gah. Seattle's close enough, thank you.

"Yeah, the Snyders' house. Single dad, eight-year-old boy. It was insta-bonding between the boys. Jonah stayed here last night, and then they went hiking today. You're going to be hearing a lot of Jonah-this and Jonah-that."

"That's nice for Madden."

"Yeah."

This is the kind of scintillating conversation Trevor and I have at pickup and drop-off.

He has said he wants to be friends, and I know he means it. Part of me wants it too, but it is so, so hard to be that good of a person.

Just then, I hear, then see, Sawyer's truck.

My pulse picks up a notch. This should be interesting.

"Elle?"

I jerk my attention back to Trevor.

"Anything else going on with Madden I need to know about?"

"Nothing I haven't mentioned." Trevor and I stay in touch by email and sometimes text.

Every time I reach out to him electronically, I think about the fact that for nearly a decade, he was texting and emailing and messaging and Skyping another woman, telling her the details of his day, his thoughts and feelings. All those parts of him I thought were for me, they never were. They belonged to her.

When I found out, I thought, *Our whole marriage is a lie.* And cried so hard and so long that my whole body hurt.

I turn away from Trevor and watch Sawyer unfold his linebacker's body from the front seat of the car. It's a riveting sight—long, strong lines and a surprising amount of grace for such a big guy.

He's very athletic. I know from personal experience. My mouth goes dry and something throbs appreciatively in my southerly regions.

Trevor's eyes follow mine.

"That's the new neighbor?"

"Yep."

The urge to tell Trevor—with words or implication or body language—that I've had sex with Sawyer is almost over-powering, but I manage to keep my mouth shut as Madden and Jonah run toward us.

Sawyer keeps his distance as the boys bound up, talking over each other in their eagerness to tell me about *the map and the salamander and the coyote and the river they waded into and and and . . .*

"Sounds like fun," Trevor says. "How would you guys like to go kayaking with me sometime soon?"

My eyes meet Sawyer's, and his eyebrows go up, just a notch. Giving Trevor the benefit of the doubt, he's probably just running with a theme, but it does sound a bit like he's trying to one-up my new neighbor.

"Wow!" Jonah says. "Dad, could we do that?"

"Don't see why not," Sawyer says easily.

Trevor strides down the steps toward Sawyer with his hand out, all jovial. "Hey there. Trevor Thomas. Great to meet you."

"Sawyer Paulson."

I bite my lip in an effort not to smile at Sawyer's cool response.

Sawyer's probably not more than five inches taller than Trevor, but he's at least fifty pounds heavier, all of it well-distributed muscle. As a result, he looms over Trevor. And I catch Trevor's wince mid-handshake, which makes it even harder not to smile.

"And this is Jonah," I say. "They're our new neighbors."

"Welcome," Trevor says.

But you don't live here anymore, I think. *You don't get to issue the welcomes anymore.*

"Madden, Helen made your favorite dinner for tonight!" Trevor says. "Spaghetti with meatballs!"

I feel only the faintest flicker of annoyance. One of the things that's been most difficult since the divorce is that when Trevor's around, I don't like either of us—him or me. Obviously, I used to love him. I loved his little quirks and foibles—was even amused by the way he dealt with his insecurities by posturing. But overnight, once I knew that he no longer loved me, my own emotions soured. And in the last year, when I've been forced to be in the same place as him, I mainly wished he would go away so I could stop feeling . . . small.

But today for some reason, I'm not feeling that way. I think it has something to do with Sawyer's presence, or maybe with the way he makes Trevor seem like the small one.

I hide a smile.

Trevor turns to me. "Elle. How's the car running? Want me to check the oil and tire pressure while I'm here?"

Okay, seriously? Even when he lived here, Trevor never

actually handled any dipstick beside his own. He knows next to nothing about cars.

Sawyer, perhaps too smart to stick around and be an audience for Trevor's display of manliness, says, "Nice to meet you, Trevor. Jonah, come on—time to go." He heads off toward his house, Jonah trailing.

"He seems like a nice enough guy," Trevor says.

Nice is completely the wrong word. *Real* is the word I'd use. Or *sure,* like sure-footed, sure of himself.

Big. Strong. Competent.

Very attractive from the rear view.

Very.

But not *nice.*

"Mmm," I say noncommittally. And then, because I suddenly feel generous, "Don't worry about the oil and tire pressure—I got it."

I can always just google the shit out of it. Or ask Sawyer for help.

I smile—actually smile—at Trevor, who looks taken aback. Which makes me realize how long it's been since I've felt like myself around him.

Not a bad feeling.

Not a bad feeling at all.

"Madden, run and change into something that's not muddy. And not sweatpants. Jeans and a T-shirt."

Madden runs upstairs.

"Don't let him drink too much soda," I tell Trevor, and leave him standing on the front stoop, waiting for Madden.

10

SAWYER

"What are you doing?"

Elle is standing in front of me, hands on hips, eyeing me quizzically over a stack of old, mostly rotted boards, the remains of our side fence.

I put Jonah on the bus an hour ago, with Madden at his side. I think Jonah would have pretty much gone to the moon as long as Madden was going to be on the spaceship. Plus, I felt a whole lot better about sending Jonah to a new school knowing someone has his back.

I thought about not sending him till next September, but I think it might be easier for him to start now so that in the fall, he knows at least a few kids already.

As soon as the bus door clanged shut behind him, I dug into my fence project—the one Elle is currently staring at suspiciously. Hell. No one warned her that I was going to rehab the fence.

"Oh, God, I'm sorry, I wasn't thinking. The Snyders asked me to fence—I assumed they'd asked you. I'm really sorry."

Her expression softens. Her hair is down. It's wavy today,

like a wheat field seen from a distance. I know how smooth it
is to the touch, how good it feels between my fingers, in my
fist.

I wish I didn't. It's distracting.

"No. No. That actually sounds—it makes sense. That
thing was—" She hesitates.

"A pile of shit?"

She smiles. Her teeth are small and even and very white,
and they were smooth under my tongue that night at Maeve's.

So distracting.

"I was just—surprised. I looked out here, and you were
ripping down the fence and I got worried about my flowers,
and—I'm sorry, too. I shouldn't have been so short with you."

I wave her apology off.

"So, um, what's the new fence gonna be like?"

"Simple cedar pickets. Really straightforward, like the old
one. But this one will be reclaimed cedar."

She tilts her head. "What's reclaimed cedar?"

"It means it's been used before, in another project. This is
from a fence that used to run along the line between two
farms in eastern Washington. I don't use new lumber. Not for
my furniture, not for my handyman projects."

Her eyes widen. "You make furniture?"

"Uh-huh."

"Wow. That's—cool. Why don't you use new lumber?"

"It's better for the earth. But I also I love handling old
things. They have history. Other people have touched and
loved them. And when I build with old lumber, that history
becomes part of what I'm building."

When I said I don't talk much, there are a couple of
exceptions. Like when I start talking about my projects.

"That's really cool. Do you know anything about the farms that the fence came from?"

"A little bit. This fence separated a dairy farm from a huge wheat farm. Kept the milk out of the cereal."

She laughs. "That sounds like a much more important job than keeping my weeds out of your backyard."

"It's *my* weeds that are running rampant." I gesture at the jungle formerly known as landscaping on the Snyders' property. "Sorry about the mess. I'll get it under control soon."

"Ah, no worries," she says, waving a hand. "Mine only looks as good as it does because I use Trevor's money to hire a landscaper every two weeks in the growing season."

Before I can think better of it, I say, "Seems like you might be better off with Trevor's money than with Trevor."

Startled, she meets my gaze. Her blue eyes are outlined in black, her lashes thick and dark. "What makes you say that?"

I'm already wishing I hadn't. The intensity of her regard makes me nervous. "I don't know. First impression."

Actually, my first impression of Trevor goes all the way back to Maeve's that night a couple of months ago, when she told me the story of what he'd done to her. Her voice was small and tight, hurt. Defeated. There she was in Maeve's, her hair a bright spot of yellow in the dimness of the bar, too beautiful to be ignored, and this asshole guy hadn't been able to see what he had straight in front of him.

I hated him even before I met him.

"You know how he struck me yesterday?" she asks, thoughtfully. "Like a little yappy dog. You know? Has to pee on everything to make sure everyone knows it's his. You took the boys hiking, so he had to say he would take them kayaking. He had to let us know that he and Helen were going to make Madden's favorite dish. And that thing about the oil and tire pressure was just him humping my leg."

I laugh.

She's staring at me.

"What?" I demand.

"I just realized I've never heard you laugh before."

That brings me back to myself with a sharp rush. "Yeah. I don't, much. Since Lucy died."

The words are out of my mouth before I can check them.

She's staring at me. "Lucy," she says, softly.

"My wife."

I watch as realization dawns, and sadness. The softening and splintering of her expression.

"I'm sorry. I'm so sorry."

"It was two years ago."

"Still." She swallows hard. "I thought you were divorced. I just assumed you were divorced."

"Yeah, well. I'm not."

I can see her struggling for words. How many people have I watched do this exact thing in the last two years? But for some reason, I don't hate it when she does it. I'm—curious, I guess. I want to know what she's going to say.

"That sucks," she says finally.

It makes me smile. Just a little. "Yeah."

"What was she like?"

Startled, I almost drop the crowbar.

"Sorry. Maybe you don't want to talk about her."

"Not really."

She nods.

There's an awkward silence. "Um, I'd better get back to this," I say, gesturing at the fence.

Her mouth flattens. For the first time, I notice she's wearing a sparkly pink color on her lips. One pearly tooth bites into the softness of the pink, and, inconveniently, I want to kiss her. Hard. Long. With a lot of tongue.

But I don't. I turn my gaze back to my work.

"Yeah. Sorry. I'll let you continue the destruction."

The warmth is gone from her voice. She turns and walks back to her house, and I'm left with the remnants of the Snyders' fence and the strong impulse to call her back. To ask her what she wants to know. To tell her whatever it is.

To cover her mouth with mine, to draw her close.

I don't . . . but I'm pretty sure I'm fighting a losing battle against myself.

11

ELLE

"So how are you getting on with Heathcliff?" Mrs. Wheeling asks me.

I'm unloading groceries into her fridge. It's three weeks since Heathcliff—Sawyer—and Jonah moved in.

Whenever I go to Safeway, I check in with Mrs. Wheeling first to see if she can use anything. She's mobile and can get there on her own, but I figure by the time I'm in my eighties I'll want to save my energy for something other than pushing a grocery cart around a poorly lit store. There are a couple of delivery services around here, but if I can save her money by tossing a few extra things in my cart every time I go to the store, I'm happy to do it. Besides, talking to Mrs. Wheeling always makes my day better.

"He seems like a nice guy." *Even if our encounters invariably end with me making a fool of myself.* "Did you know he makes furniture?"

"Yes! Do you want to see what he built me?"

"Built you?"

She rises from the kitchen table and headed for the stairs,

obviously assuming I'm going to follow her—which I do.

Her bedroom sports newly installed built-in bookshelves on both walls.

"So I can keep more books!"

"That's wonderful."

The shelves are simple but beautiful, painted white, filled with her romance novels.

"You know what the best part was?" she asks.

I shake my head.

"It took him a day and a half, and the whole time he was working I got to bring him things. Glasses of water, and plates of food. And I never wanted to interrupt him, so I just would stand behind him or off to the side and watch him work for a little while. That man. He is—" She smacks her lips.

"Mrs. Wheeling, you are a dirty old woman."

"I know!" she says gleefully.

I don't mention that I use every break from interviewing and writing to study him while he works on the side fence, taking in the glint of sunlight on his black hair, the way he backhands sweat from his brow, the way he scowls at an uncooperative board.

I don't want to draw her laser focus to my inappropriate obsession with my neighbor's broad shoulders or make her suspect that I am now regularly fantasizing about inviting him in for a glass of cold water and a plate of cookies . . .

Also, *stalker* much?

Since Jonah and Sawyer moved in, Jonah and Madden have been inseparable except when they're asleep in their own beds and during the two weekends that Madden was with his father.

And yet somehow, although I've seen Sawyer outside

plenty of times at work, I have avoided conversation with him, except for that one interaction the day he started demolition of the fence. The one where we were, briefly, kind of —friends.

Seems like you might be better off with Trevor's money than with Trevor.

Isn't that something you'd say to a friend?

Except then I had to go and push too far about his wife.

Big mistake. He shut down completely.

I rewrite that conversation frequently, imagining that I had left well-enough alone. Although I don't really know what I would do if Sawyer and I were friends.

Spend even more time lusting, I suppose.

Mrs. Wheeling has resumed her new favorite topic, her gaze dreamy, looking for all the world like a moony middle-school girl. "He really is a work of art. A renaissance sculpture. His forearms alone are worth the price of admission. Well, that's kind of a given, since he didn't charge me for the shelves."

"He didn't charge you for the shelves?"

She shakes her head. "He said he has a senior citizen price, and it's *free.*"

I'm sure that's not true, but Mrs. Wheeling is holding on to her house and her independence by the skin of her teeth, and there's no way she could afford the going rate for built-in bookshelves. Still, to give a day and a half's labor to her, when I know he has all that furniture to build—and maintenance to do on his own property—it's pretty damn admirable.

"He's a good guy," Mrs. Wheeling says.

She's watching me with a calculating expression.

"I'm sure he is."

"He's a good guy, and he's a good dad—"

"How do you know?" I say it teasingly, but I'm not fooling either of us: I'm insanely curious.

"I see him with Jonah. He's always showing him how to do things. Measure, cut, join. You have to have patience to show a kid how to do things. Me, I used to try to teach my girls to bake, but I'd end up ripping the measuring spoons out of their hands because they were so slow or they'd do it wrong and spill stuff or they were sloppy and I was afraid they'd ruin the recipe. I think it takes a saint to teach a kid to cook or build."

I'm smiling, because I've been there with Madden—trying to teach him something I know he needs to learn, but desperately wanting to wrench whatever it is away from him so we can get it done sometime this century.

"I'm just trying to tell you, Elle, Sawyer Paulson is a good guy, a good dad, and a damn fine specimen of manhood."

"But I'm not in the market for any of those things." God knows it will be a long time before I'm ready to believe anything a man tells me, other than that he wants to have sex.

Mrs. Wheeling raises one sparse white eyebrow. "So you say, my dear. So you say. But sometimes you need to ride a different horse before you can be ready to sell the old one."

My mouth falls open. "Is that actually a saying?"

"No." She laughs—somewhere between a giggle and a cackle. I find myself hoping I will be as uninhibited in all respects as Mrs. Wheeling when I am in my eighties. "I made it up! But I think it fits, don't you? No pun intended."

"Mrs. *Wheeling.*"

"Just saying, as my grandkids would say these days. Just saying, my dear."

12

ELLE

A few days after my conversation with the delightful Mrs. Wheeling, I'm folding Madden's summer clothes into his dresser, stowing the winter ones on a high shelf in his closet, when my cellphone vibrates. I set down the T-shirts I'm holding and retrieve the phone.

It's the school. These calls always make my heart beat faster. The last few have been, respectively, a sprained wrist, a broken finger, and projectile vomit in math class.

"This is Elle."

"Ms. Dunning. This is Jim McKibben. I'm the principal at Oak Ridge Elementary. Madden is fine—"

Why do people think that's a reassuring thing to say? My heart is going a million miles a minute.

"—but we need you to come to school. There's been a series of incidents this week in the classroom, and we've just gotten to the bottom of it, and Madden is one of the perpetrators."

"Incidents? Perpetrators?"

Madden has always been an angel at school. He's a

natural people-pleaser. Even when he was at his most sullen at home, after Trevor left, his third-grade teacher, Mr. Ketotzi, said he was doing fine at school. He saved the bad mood for me, apparently.

So at first I think, *Are you* sure *we're talking about Madden?*

The words almost come out of my mouth, but I stop them just in time.

"I think it would be easier to explain if you came into school," Mr. McKibben says.

"Can't you tell me anything else?"

"He and another student have been harassing Mr. Ketotzi."

"Harassing?"

I sound like a broken record, but that's how shocked I am.

"Like I said, this isn't the first incident; this is just the first time we've been able to figure out who's responsible. Come on in, Ms. Dunning, and we'll talk."

I hang up and jump in my car. I make it to the school in record time. The secretary gives me a look somewhere between disapproval and pity—I think they get training for that—and tells me to go ahead into the principal's office.

Mr. McKibben faces out from his desk, a sixty-something man with close-cropped hair and a distinctly military bearing. Sitting in front of him are Madden and Jonah.

"Ms. Dunning. Thank you so much for coming in. We're just waiting for—"

The door swings open and Sawyer stands in the doorway. He's wearing dust-covered work clothes—Carhartt khakis and heavy leather boots and a gray T-shirt—and his hair is full of dust, too. I imagine crossing the room and brushing my hand over the soft waves. I squelch the thought.

"Ah, Mr. Paulson. Come in. Here, let me grab a couple more chairs from—"

"Don't bother." Sawyer crosses his arms and leans against the back wall of the office. Everything about his appearance and body language says that this is a waste of his valuable time. He looks like a guy who spent his own fair share of time in the principal's office as a kid.

I suspect his attitude won't help our case. I should be irritated by it, but I'm not. I'm amused. And intrigued. He looks like the kind of boy I fantasized about in high school, the bad boy who'd never give me the time of day but who I nevertheless daydreamed would one day lure me under the football bleachers for a make-out session. Plus, I know exactly how masterful this particular bad boy is with fingers, mouth—er, yes, that, too. My body gives a silent squawk of approval.

"Ms. Dunning?" Mr. McKibben inquires, and it takes me a minute to figure out he's asking if I want a chair.

"I'll take one," I say, blushing ferociously. "Thank you so much."

Mr. McKibben exits and returns with two chairs. I sit. Sawyer remains against the wall. He doesn't look at me, or at Jonah.

Mr. McKibben clears his throat and folds his hands. "This week, there have been several incidents of either harassment or insubordination in the classroom, but we haven't been able to get the students to tell us who's responsible until today. Today we told the students that they would all miss recess for a week unless someone came forward, and someone did. I won't name names, but this student identified Jonah and Madden as the ones behind the incidents, the ringleaders."

"And what were the incidents?" I ask, trying to catch

Madden's eye. I feel like I'll be able to read so much more about the situation in his face if he'll only look at me.

"On Monday, all the students in the class began calling Mr. Ketotzi *Mrs. Ketotzi.*"

Madden's eyes meet mine finally, then fall away. I bite my lip. He raises his blond head again, and I see defiance on his small features.

Huh. What's that about? He's guilty *and* self-righteous.

"On Tuesday, when Mr. Ketotzi asked the students to line up girls first, the boys lined up first." Mr. McKibben ticks off the offense on his index finger.

"On Wednesday, someone replaced Mr. Ketotzi's blue-and-green fleece jacket with a pink one." A second finger.

I wince.

"And then today, the students refused to pick teams in P.E." Mr. McKibben abandons his fingers and crosses his arms. "Taken by themselves, these are all fairly minor infractions, but they're disruptive, they waste time, and they undermine Mr. Ketotzi's authority. It's disrespectful, plain and simple, and all the students have been told quite clearly after each of the incidents that it's not acceptable behavior. So we're going to ask Jonah and Madden to stay home from school tomorrow."

"You're suspending them?" I demand, before I can think better of it.

"Yes. For one day. And we'd like them to perform community service. Every day after school for a week, next week, emptying the trash cans in all the classrooms."

My stomach hurts like I'm the one who's in trouble. I never got called to the principal's office, and I'm not liking the feeling, even in the parental role.

"Also, Mr. Paulson?"

Sawyer's expression barely flickers. He must have made administrators miserable when he was a kid.

"Madden has been at this school for several years and has never given us the slightest cause for concern about his behavior. If Jonah continues to be a bad influence on him, we'll have to separate them into different classrooms next year."

Jumping to conclusions much?

Sawyer's eyebrows rise and a muscle moves, a visible knot, at his jaw. One fist tightens. "Noted," he says stiffly. He seems, I observe, like a guy who's used to taking it on the chin, whether he deserves it or not. But I'm also watching Jonah, and he's shrinking in his chair.

"No," I say, without thinking it through.

"Excuse me?" Mr. McKibben asks.

"I don't buy it."

Sawyer's mouth is open.

Mr. McKibben seems to be struggling for words.

"I've spent almost as much time the last three weeks with Jonah as I have with my own son. And I like to think I'm a pretty good judge of character. Jonah's not a bad influence. So whatever happened here—it's not what you think."

Jonah sits up a little straighter in his seat.

Mr. McKibben opens his mouth, but before he can speak, Madden's voice, small but strong, cuts through the stale air of the small office.

"It wasn't Jonah's idea. It was mine. It was because of Junie." Madden pronounces it "a-cuz," which he's done since he was little.

"Who's Junie?" I ask.

"She's in our class. Her parents thought she was a boy when she was born, and we thought she was a boy when she was in first grade. But she's actually a girl. And Mr. Ketotzi makes Junie line up with the boys."

It's my turn to gape.

Mr. McKibben looks equally gobsmacked. It's safe to say that this is news to him.

"And when we choose teams in gym, Mr. Ketotzi makes us choose Junie with the boys, not the girls," Madden says, and I can tell he's almost crying from frustration, his little voice tight with righteous rage.

Mr. McKibben recovers his ability to speak. "Did you try to talk to Mr. K about it?" he asks the boys.

Madden and Jonah exchange glances. I think Madden's asking Jonah, in some eight-year-old language beyond words, for permission to speak freely. They seem to reach a decision, and Madden nods. "After he made Junie be a boy in gym, we told him we didn't think it was fair. But he asked if we were little girls, too, and that's why we were friends with Junie, and then he told us to sit down and be quiet. Jonah said he was going to tell Mr. McKibben and Mr. Ketotzi said, 'Mr. McKibben and I have been friends since 1980. Who do you think he's going to listen to?' so we didn't."

The office is so quiet you can hear the click of typing in the outer lobby, and the murmur of conversation next door in the counselor's office.

Sawyer's and my gazes swing to Mr. McKibben. Red has risen to his cheekbones, and he's wincing. He opens his mouth, closes it, opens it again, then shakes his head. "I would never let a friendship interfere with my ability to do my job. You have to believe that." He turns a pleading expression on Sawyer and me. "Washington State law is on Junie's side, and I would have been, too." He sighs. "You know what? Let's start over. If you would be so kind as to bear with me. Because Elle, you're absolutely right. I was in the wrong on this. Boys, I should have asked to hear your story. Jonah, I'm sorry I distrusted you and didn't give you the benefit of the doubt. Mr. Paulson, I apologize—"

Sawyer nods. "Accepted."

There is the slightest lift at one corner of Sawyer's mouth. That almost-smile on him is like a full-on beam from most guys. He catches my glance and the smile reaches all the way to his eyes, then drops away as he turns to the boys. He addresses them sternly.

"Jonah? Madden? Next time you think a teacher needs to be punished for their behavior, you need to tell Mr. McKibben or Elle and me first. Got it?"

The boys nod like bobble-head dolls, eyes huge.

"And you guys need to lay off harassing Mr. Ketotzi, since he's going to be getting an earful from Mr. McKibben. Right, Mr. McKibben?"

Mr. McKibben smiles ruefully. "Absolutely."

We all draw deep breaths for the first time since we convened.

"So—no suspension?" I ask.

"Doesn't really seem to fit the crime," Mr. McKibben says with a sigh. "How about the boys do trash duty this afternoon —just one day—to remind them that it's not a good idea to take justice against teachers into their own hands?"

"Seems fair," I say, looking to Sawyer, who gives another of those curt male nods.

"Grab one of the big rolling trash bins from the cafeteria

and go from room to room emptying the classroom cans. The custodian will lock up behind you."

I stand and Sawyer pushes off the wall, and I say, "Come on, boys. We've got work to do."

Sawyer and I follow the boys out into the hallway.

"Hey," he says.

I turn. He's standing very still, and his face is serious.

"That was real good of you to stand up for Jonah. You didn't have to do that. And you probably saved my ass, too. I could tell it was one of those situations where I was gonna make it worse as soon as I opened my mouth."

I smile. "I doubt that."

"Never been great with authority figures," he says, lifting one big shoulder in an eloquent shrug. "Anyway, thank you."

"It seemed like the *neighborly* thing to do." I lift one eyebrow at the word we've settled on to describe things between us, thinking, even as I say it, how inadequate it seems. "And it's true. Jonah's a sweet kid. I meant every word."

"Well. Thanks." He starts to follow the boys, then stops and steps back toward me. "I was thinking. Jonah goes to this summer program. It's an outdoor adventure camp, six nights, for boys in third and fourth grades. Rock climbing, kayaking, hiking, camping, caving, you name it. My friend Chase knows the guys who lead it, so I think I could get Madden a place, if you're interested, even though it's full. It's in August. Jonah would be glad to have him."

"I'd love that. Madden would love that."

"Okay. I'll, um, make it so."

His gaze lingers on my face for a moment, harkening back to the way he looked at me in Maeve's right before he kissed me, flooding me with unexpected heat. I can practically feel the touch of his hand on my face.

Then he steps away, hurrying after the boys, who have already claimed a trash bin from the cafeteria and are pushing it down the hall at an unholy speed. I follow behind, more slowly. I'm trying to put together the pieces of how I feel. Sawyer's offer made me feel oddly giddy, like he'd invited me into his life. And yet, what I learned over the wreckage of our side fence made me feel, more than ever, like I can't let myself have any feelings for Sawyer. He meant exactly what he implied that night in Maeve's—he's not available.

He's still in love with his late wife.

And the thing is, when Trevor left, I promised myself that no matter what I did, I'd never let myself fall for a guy who was in love with a ghost again.

13

SAWYER

The day after the boys were called to the principal's office, it rains, hard enough that I have to put fence work on hold. Which is fine, because I need to put in some good time on the first Reclaimed House furniture order and start in on some of the indoor reno projects, if I want to get the house rehabbed sometime in this century.

I decide I'll do the rehab work in the morning and then start in on coffee tables—which are outselling all my other products—in the afternoon.

The first order of business is the wall-to-wall carpeting in the living room. I think it was probably an attractive blue-gray when it was first installed, but it is more of a gray-brown now. A good cleaning would take care of that problem, but it's also worn nearly to the weave in the heavily trafficked spots near the front door and the kitchen. So I start in one corner, pulling it back. Dust and something worse, some mildewy odor, rise as I separate it from the pad, and I have to go out to the garage to find goggles and a dust mask.

I'm hoping against hope—because it does happen some-times—to discover that the crappy carpet was laid over hard-wood floor, but no such luck. There's just subflooring, although, thankfully, that's in good condition. I set to work tearing up the carpet, the pad, the liner, and the tack strips, heaping the discards in a pile by the door. I'll need to make a dump run later.

It's dull, dusty work, but it's also brain-dead, so I can muse on what happened yesterday at school. When I walked into that principal's office, it threw me right back to my childhood and all the times I was the one in that hot seat. I wasn't a bad kid, just easily distracted, at least in elementary school and junior high. Lots of pranks, not so different than the ones Madden and Jonah had orchestrated, although not usually for such a noble cause. Mine were more of the variety of ordering a hundred pizzas to be sent to the teachers' lounge and billed to the high school's activities account.

I've been sort of vaguely aware of this whole gender thing going on, kids going by a gender that's different from the one they started with, but this was the first time it had really crossed my path in a personal way. I hadn't given it too much thought before, but if Jonah can be cool with it, I sure as fuck can. And I'm proud of my kid. If anything—and I kept my mouth shut, not wanting to get into it with Mr. McKibben—I think the principal had things backwards. It's not Jonah being a bad influence on Madden, it's Madden being a great influ-ence on Jonah. But whatever. The point is, those kids are clearly going to be friends, which means . . .

Well, it means that there won't be any way for me to stay away from Elle.

Plus, I don't want to stay away from her. She was pretty spectacular yesterday, standing up for my kid (and hers, too, of course, but that's par for the course, right?). She's petite, but she packs a punch, and yesterday when she lit into McKibben, her cheeks were pink, her hair coming loose in strands from a ponytail, and her eyes blazing. She was breathing hard, as one does in these situations, and I couldn't take my eyes off her. When we left the office together, I wanted to kiss the hell out of her.

It's time to admit it: I want to have sex with her again. In pretty much the worst way.

I try not to give too much thought to the question of why, of all people, she's the one who makes me contemplate a redo...

Instead, I haul armfuls of carpet and rubber mat and those goddamn prickly little tack strips down to the garage. I pause to make myself a ham sandwich, then eat it standing up in the living room, thinking about next steps. I want to find some oak flooring. There's a place I like in Seattle that salvages and resells reclaimed flooring, and I've gotten great stuff there in the past—boards with a lot of wear left in them, with their tongue-and-groove still intact so they're relatively easy to install without a lot of extra joint-cutting. That would be the easiest. Or I could look for something with more of a story—boards coming out of a house where a family lived happily for years, or from an old dance floor, whatever. We'll see. Depends how much time and energy I have.

I head down to my garage workshop and survey the stack of materials I've collected for the furniture work. If I do them in parallel, I have enough space to construct three tables pretty quickly, box them, and ship them. The catalog company does the collateral—the assembly instructions and all that.

I whistle as I work.

I haven't whistled in a long, long time.

14

ELLE

I t's Friday afternoon. Madden is up in his room packing a bag for a weekend with his dad. I'm working on a profile of a local nurse midwife, sitting at the dining room table with my laptop.

Well, I'm supposed to be working on that profile.

I've got a second file open, and I'm working on my super-secret project. It's so secret that it will probably never see the light of day. It's a book about divorce. At first it was just me writing down things that happened, like notes to myself so I wouldn't forget, but then I realized it had turned into kind of a memoir crossed with a self-help book.

It was so damn therapeutic to write about how it felt to find out the truth. How I nudged the mouse on Trevor's computer one day while searching for a tax form I needed, and his computer sprang to life, open to a long Facebook Messenger exchange between him and Helen. How I tried not to read it, but words kept jumping off the screen at me. *How much longer do you think until you can tell her?*

Not too much longer.

When I saw that, I thought about movies where the Other Woman kept wanting her lover to leave his wife, and he kept not doing it. *Maybe this is like that,* I thought. *Maybe if I don't say anything, eventually Trevor will just come back to me.*

Then I realized how pathetic that was, keeping quiet and hoping I'd win in the end, and I couldn't do it. I had to tell him what I'd seen. But even then, there was a part of me that hoped he'd tell me it didn't mean what it looked like.

That didn't happen.

I cried for weeks before I made the decision to stop crying and embrace who I was now. A single mom sharing custody of her great son, a woman who was lucky enough to have a career to come back to when her marriage fell apart. I didn't make myself sound like a hero. I wrote it as truthfully as I could, detailing how the first days after I stopped crying I still felt like I was dragging around a corpse behind me (except the corpse was me, my actual body; it just felt that heavy). And then gradually I got lighter and started to actually enjoy myself. Until finally some things—like Trevor's yappiness— were funny.

Today I'm writing about the night I slept with Sawyer.

Because weird as it is to say, I think something turned around that night. I reclaimed another piece of myself, the sexy part. The fun part. And even if nothing ever happens again with Sawyer, I'll always know he gave me that back.

Writing about that night means, of course, thinking about that night, and I find myself dreamily recalling the moment when he reached his hand out and brushed his thumb across my lower lip.

That man has the off switch for my common sense. If he actually had touched me the other day after our meeting in

Mr. McKibben's office, I probably would have ended up making out with him in a deserted elementary school classroom. Good thing he didn't.

I write a few more lines, then sit back and admire my handiwork.

Hattie thinks I should try to get it published. She's read some bits and she says it's really touching and sometimes downright hilarious. But I told her that no one wants to read a book about a suburban divorced thirty-something. Anyway, remember *Eat Pray Love*? There are a million memoir-meets-self-help books about stuff, including divorce. So I just keep adding bits, mostly for my own enjoyment.

I get up and step over to the window, ostensibly just to stretch and take a break, but actually because I need to enjoy the view. This ritual has become part of my writing routine.

Sawyer, cordless power tool in one hand, is standing on a ladder on his side of the fence, attaching lattice panels to the top of our side of the fence.

The fence is a gorgeous piece of work.

So is he.

The sun is touching his dark hair, which gleams. The fierce look of concentration on his face sends a pleasant shiver up my spine. His T-shirt stretches taut across his pecs and biceps as he moves and shifts, and his forearms are bare —well muscled, dusted with dark hair, beautiful to watch in action.

I should stop acting like a stalker and go have a conversation with him. I force myself to move away from behind the dining room curtain and head out into the yard. As I emerge from the house, he shuts off the electric screwdriver and raises his head, nodding in greeting.

"Hey," I call.

"Hey."

It's funny how I've stopped hearing his curtness as rudeness or lack of interest. The more I get to know him, the more I understand that he's just like that. Not a lot of words. But he's a good listener, and he cares about other people.

I approach the fence and touch the lattice panel next to where he's working. The boards of the main fence, beautiful but rugged in much the same way as Sawyer himself, run horizontal. "This is a sweet fence. But I thought you said it was going to be plain old pickets, like the old one?"

He frowns. "If I built a picket fence, there'd be a front and a back side, and one of us would have to look at the back."

"Why didn't you just face the back toward me?"

He shrugs. "Didn't want to. After I didn't ask your permission to tear the fence down, didn't seem right."

"Aw," I say. "That's awfully nice."

Faint color rises in his cheeks, and he waves me off. "Thought about doing it as a good-neighbor fence, where the pickets alternate so neither of us sees the back, but I don't like the way those look. So I did it this way."

"And the lattice?"

The lattice strikes me as very un-Sawyer-like. It's beautiful, ornamental, but it doesn't fit his no-nonsense style.

"Thought you'd like it," he says, with another of his eloquent shrugs.

It's hard to express exactly how that makes me feel. Warm and fuzzy, and also a little terrified. Because this is a guy who —with a few words and a throwaway gesture—can make me feel like I actually matter.

Pretty much everything that's happened to me in the last

year has made me feel like I don't. Trevor's actions this year have not only hurt my feelings in the short term but also made me question every time I ever believed or trusted him, every time I ever felt safe and secure in his affections. Trevor did a bang-up job of making me feel like I didn't matter at all, and never really had.

And then Sawyer Paulson goes and builds a few lattice panels and all of a sudden I go all soft and gooey.

Hmm. I may be in trouble.

I can't even run away, because he *lives here.*

"Don't you like it?" he asks.

There is a wariness on his face that I can't stand, like the expression of a dog that has been beaten one too many times.

I sigh. "Sawyer. I love it."

15

SAWYER

Huh. So apparently, without realizing it, I've been building this fence for Elle. As soon as I asked the question—*Don't you like it?*—even before I found myself waiting eagerly for her answer, I knew.

I've been showing off for her.

Two-sided fence? For Elle. Horizontal pickets, with their fidgety fit into the posts? For Elle. Lattice, which has taken me freaking forever to construct one panel at a time? For Elle.

One reclaimed cedar fence, ten times fancier than the situation requires?

For Elle.

Basically, that fence is like a male peacock displaying its tail feathers.

I'm definitely going to have sex with her again.

I probably should have known I was going to go after round two when I got home from Maeve's right after our alley encounter. I jogged up the stairs—Jonah was sleeping at his grandparents' house—brushed my teeth, removed my belt, jeans, and shoes, and got into bed. I was expecting to pretty much pass out, what with the whiskey and how hard I'd come—standing up—a mere half hour ago, but that wasn't what happened.

By all rights, sex should have been the last thing on my mind, except maybe a quick mental review—you know, storing the images up for future spank-bank material.

Instead, I was imagining how it would be if there were a next time.

What would it have been like if I fucked her from behind? Her hands up on the wall? Or bent her over the edge of a bed?

Or, what if we did it lying down? Slow. Face-to-face, so I could watch what her face did when she made those noises. When she pulsed and spasmed around me.

Spoiler: I ended up with my dick out, a palm full of lube, and a chest covered with cum. So in that sense, she was the first woman since Lucy died who got me off twice in one night.

Yes, that made me feel guilty as shit. Which is part of why I made myself put her out of my head for a while after that.

Until she showed up at my front door. That was when I got my second strong set of clues that I wasn't done with her. That I still had designs on her.

And if that wasn't information enough, there was the ordeal of hiking in the woods after seeing her with the spatula in her hand.

And watching her go toe-to-toe with McKibben.

Anyway, the point is, now I've quit denying what I should have known all along.

I don't have time to act on my newfound knowledge,

though, because just then a familiar car pulls up outside Elle's house. Madden's dad's Camry.

Elle turns to look in the direction of my gaze and sighs heavily. "Wish me luck."

I watch Mr. Yap step out of the driver's seat. "Have you tried bacon treats? I hear they're great for house training."

She laughs, shoots me an appreciative look, and heads over to her front yard to greet Trevor. There's someone else emerging from the car now, a tall, willowy raven-haired woman.

Oh, shit. I have to assume she's Trevor's high school girl-friend and fiancée, and my heart picks up in sympathy for Elle.

Elle's step hitches—she's seen the other woman, and she hesitates a moment before continuing. She's got to be feeling pretty miserable right now. Trevor on his own is bad enough, but having your kid picked up by the woman who stole your husband . . .?

No fun.

I watch through the lattice—stalker-neighbor-style—as the woman approaches Elle with a smile and extends her hand to shake. The other woman is wearing a short skirt and a white V-neck shirt that reveals epic quantities of cleavage. There's no denying she's a beautiful woman, but not my type —she looks wound too tight. I know, though, that she's the kind of woman who makes other women crazy—makes them go home and pinch their invisible belly fat and schedule hair-cuts and makeovers. I know because that used to happen to Lucy sometimes. She'd come home from the gym or a PTO meeting and stand in front of the mirror and fidget with her hair and look completely defeated.

But you're beautiful!

Not like so-and-so, though.

You're better!

You're just saying that because you're my husband.

I'm saying it because it's true.

I could usually make her believe it. She'd abandon her hairbrush or her eyeliner and come with me into the bedroom, and I'd finish convincing her.

I close my eyes against the pain, but when I open them again, Helen is tossing her hair and laughing.

Possessed by some impulse I can't quite name, I set down my tools and head around the fence and into Elle's yard.

Trevor, Helen, and Elle are standing in a small clump. Elle looks miserable, her shoulders slumped inward like she's trying to disappear.

"Hey," I call out.

Trevor looks up. An irritated expression crosses his face. Excellent. Ticking Trevor off is my new favorite sport.

"Hi, Simon," Trevor says.

"Sawyer," Elle bites out.

"Hi, Travis," I reply cheerfully.

Elle doesn't correct me, and Travis bristles. 2–0, me.

"This is Helen," Elle tells me, indicating the other woman. "She and Trevor are getting married in a couple of weeks."

"Which reminds me," Helen says. Her voice is husky and rich. Her eyes are dark, and rimmed with smoky makeup. She would definitely have made Lucy crazy. "We haven't gotten an RSVP from you."

She's a sadist.

Elle opens her mouth, but Helen interrupts. "We understand if it's too difficult," she says sympathetically.

No, pityingly.

I can't help it—I jump in. I tell myself I'm doing it for Lucy and all the other women in the world who feel intimidated by Helen, but the truth is, I can't stand the smugness on Helen's face, or the despair on Elle's.

"That's my fault. I've been trying to change some plans around. But we're in. For sure. Right, babe?"

I put my arm around Elle's slim waist and drop a casual kiss on her mouth.

Or, that's my plan.

I forget, though, about the power of Elle.

I feel her breath on my lips. A slight shiver goes through her body, and I remember the way she responded to me that night in the alley. And even though the kiss lasts only a millisecond, I smell her skin and her flowery shampoo, and I taste her mouth.

I go from zero to sixty.

I want to tease her lips apart, find her tongue with mine, turn her into my arms, and take everything I want from her.

It's Elle who keeps things from getting out of control. She gives a small, light laugh and slips her hand between us, pushing gently on my chest. "That's right. We're in," she tells Trevor and Helen.

I have to give her kudos—it's seamless. You can't tell I caught her totally off guard.

"Hi, Daddy."

Madden is suddenly at my elbow. Did he see me kiss his mom? He doesn't seem unsettled or perturbed in the slightest. He hugs his dad, gives his stepmother-to-be a cool glance, and accepts her pat on the head.

"Well," says Helen, "we're delighted we'll have you both

there."

She sounds disappointed, and I want to do a victory lap. Or maybe that's because of the sensation that rushed through my body when my mouth touched Elle's, like flame leaping from paper to tinder.

"Run and get your bag," Elle tells Madden. "It's in the living room."

Madden runs. Trevor is staring at Elle like she's grown a third arm. "I hope you'll be careful of Madden's feelings," he says prissily.

When Elle said he was a small dog, I'd thought of him as a Yorkshire terrier, but right now I'm picturing him as a Maltese with its fluffy white hair in a bow on top of its head.

I have to work really hard not to laugh.

"I'm always careful with Madden's feelings," Elle says mildly.

"This could be confusing for him, I'd think," Trevor says.

What a dick! So the rules are, he's allowed to bust up his marriage and turn his kid's life upside down, but she has to be celibate till the end of time? I almost get up in the guy's face, but Elle beats me to it.

"Would that be more or less confusing than his father leaving his mother because he cheated on her with his high school girlfriend?" Elle inquires.

Trevor's face goes blank. So does Helen's.

I fail, completely, to keep a straight face.

Elle slips her small, warm hand into mine and leans back against me.

It feels way better than scoring a point against Trevor.

It's more like when you level up in an arcade game and the numbers roll up, over and over, in celebration.

16

ELLE

Oh my God Oh my God Oh my God.

I recover my senses just enough that when Madden comes outside, I step away from Sawyer, pulling my hand out of his. As irritated as I am with Trevor, I know he's right. We can't make things any more complicated for Madden than they already are. I have no intention of involving him in Sawyer's and my ploy—which is all it is, of course. Luckily, I'm pretty sure Madden didn't see Sawyer lay one on me.

But *Oh my God.*

It was the most innocent of kisses. It was barely even a kiss, the lightest touch of lips to lips.

Yet I'm buzzing all over, every inch of me begging for more.

A moment before the kiss, I'd wanted to sink through the ground. Helen was standing there, looking magnificent and being understanding in the most condescending way. Then Sawyer swooped in and saved my pride.

"Have a good weekend, bud," I tell Madden, leaning down

to hug him tight. I steer him gently toward Helen and Trevor, stroke his hair, and let him go.

He's so little, still, and it always hurts to watch him walk away, even when he turns back and gives me his shy smile and a wave.

As Trevor pulls away from the curb, I turn to Sawyer. "You didn't have to do that."

He shrugs. "You went to bat for me the other day in McKibben's office. I owed you one."

Ouch.

I mean, I wasn't flattering myself that he'd kissed me because he'd been overcome by my sex appeal, but still. *I owed you one.* Yeesh.

"No," he says, seeing my expression. "I didn't mean it that way. I—" He stops, and I can see him searching for the right words. "I wanted to help. I like you and Trevor's a dick, and Helen's a twat—sorry—"

"At least your degrading language is spread around, gender-wise," I say, unable to hide a smile.

He sighs. "I don't know why I did it, I just did it. And I'm sorry if I made things complicated for you."

To be honest, I kind of like that. *I don't know why I did it, I just did it.* I mean, who knows why the hell they do half the stuff they do. And maybe he did it just because he wanted to, which—well, if so, that's awfully nice to think about.

"It's fine," I say. "I was going to ask you to come to the wedding with me anyway, probably. I was just going to have you come as my friend. Or, you know, just a 'plus one.' Leave things a little more . . . ambiguous. Now they think we're sleeping together, and it just gives Trevor something to be a dick about. But that's fine. I can handle him."

"That you can," he says, his mouth lifting. "I wanted to see a mic drop."

"I sounded a lot feistier than I felt," I admit. "She makes me feel like checking in a mirror for food in my teeth. I've always been jealous of her. From the very beginning—I mean, way back when they broke up and he started dating me."

"She dumped him?"

I heave a ginormous sigh, remembering. "Yeah. Should have seen it, right? Total rebound setup. He said he was over her, but I secretly worried he wasn't. I obsessed about stuff, saw meaning in all sorts of things he did, like saving tickets from plays they'd attended together or liking songs she'd introduced him to. Once Trevor and I were married and had a kid, and things seemed so good between us, I told myself that I'd been wrong about all that, paranoid. But she didn't go away. Her name would come up randomly. Or one of us would unearth an artifact or a photo from their time together, and I'd go into a jealousy spiral. No matter what he said, I was never quite convinced that he didn't still think about her and want her. That he didn't still think of her as the one who'd gotten away. And Trevor's parents were totally in love with her. They asked about her all the time. What was she up to, all that stuff. And he always knew the answer. Which used to make me crazy, but I could never quite bring myself to ask him to unfriend her on Facebook—it just seemed so petty, you know? I was the wife. She was a Facebook friend. Or that's what I tried to tell myself. But I was right," I say softly. "In the end, I was right. My instincts told me he still loved her, and I was right. I learned a lot about trusting myself."

I have to catch my breath. I really don't like to talk about what happened. It's just too humiliating. But Sawyer—well, I always talk too much when he's around. Maybe because he doesn't. Or maybe because he listens.

"He's not a dick," Sawyer says thoughtfully. "He's a cheap hot pink dildo."

That makes me laugh. He may not be a man of many words, but he uses them to good effect. "Well, yes," I say.

"And she's not all that. You're way prettier."

I swing my gaze to his face. He's looking down at me with an expression I recognize. It's the same one he wore in Maeve's right before he reached out a hand and brushed my lower lip. Right before he kissed me.

If I don't do anything to stop him, he's going to kiss me again.

A million thoughts go through my head. Some of them are little more than cries of, *Bad idea! Don't do it, Dunning!*

Some of them are a little more coherent. *He's your neighbor. It would be so easy for this to get messy.*

You could ruin everything for Jonah and Madden if this goes wrong.

And the loudest and sanest of all:

He's still in love with his late wife.

"Someone needs to remind you that you're beautiful."

He says it almost under his breath, like he's talking to himself.

Then he tips my chin and says, his eyes locked on mine, "You're beautiful."

He leans in, cups my head, and lowers his mouth to mine.

Her mouth opens for me. Right away. I don't even have to coax her lips apart with my tongue. And for some reason, that gets me going. How willing she is. How eager.

She fits her body against mine with a breathy sigh, raising herself onto her toes, pressing the vee of her jeans against my thigh, her breasts against my ribs. She yields completely, her mouth soft and sweet and hot, her hands grabby, and where her sex nudges against me through two layers of fabric, I can feel heat radiating. Blood rushes into my dick so fast I get light-headed. Involuntarily, I push my erection against the softness of her belly.

She breaks the kiss, drawing a breath that's more like a gasp.

"Shh," I say. "What will the neighbors think?"

She covers her face with her hands and draws back, inserting a small amount of too-cool space between us.

"Wow," she says between her fingers. When she drops her hands, her face is flushed. Her breath comes fast, in little pants, her breasts heaving. It makes my dick—already hard—even more ridiculously rigid. I'm tangled up in my briefs, longing desperately to get free and—

Well, and everything.

"And yikes," she adds, with a small, embarrassed laugh, and takes another step back.

"Should we go inside?" I gesture at her house. And then mine. Offering her choices.

Her gaze follows my hand. She frowns. When she looks up at me, I can see that I've lost her.

"Sawyer," she says.

"What?"

"You don't do repeats."

She's right, of course. But I can't make myself care, not now, with the taste of her on my lips and the sensation of holding her still rushing through my nerve endings.

"I would make an exception. I've wanted a repeat since that night outside Maeve's."

"Me, too." Her eyes are bright. Hopeful. "It was good, wasn't it? So good?"

The pleasure of hearing her say that swells my head and my dick. I was pretty sure it was good for her, too—I didn't think she could fake that kind of reaction—but it's always nice to hear it. But then her face falls. "The thing is, Sawyer, you have really good reasons not to do repeats. I mean, your wife and all. I can tell you still love her."

I don't try to deny it.

"And also, I mean, this is kind of an effed-up situation. We're neighbors. And our kids are friends. And—" She hesitates. "I'm still putting things back together, too. I mean, I'm not in love with Trevor anymore, but I'm also not, like, over what happened, obviously. So I guess I'm saying—I don't know what I'm saying. I'm saying—"

"Are you saying no?" If so, I want her to have to say it, straight and simple, out loud. But I don't think that's what she's saying. Not exactly.

"It's just—I think I'd end up getting hurt, you know? Because I'm guessing you don't want anything, you know, serious, and—I don't, either, but—I know myself and I'm the kind of person who just—if we end up having sex, and it's not just strangers at a bar one time, but if we were, like, friends with benefits—it would get complicated."

I could kiss her to shut her up, I could kiss her hard and sweep all the rational thoughts out of her head, but I let her talk because she's talking sense and because, truth? I like it when she does this, when she says what's in her head.

"And I do like you, Sawyer, I think you're a good dad and a really, really good guy, the kind who builds his elderly neighbor free bookshelves and would construct a fence that looks attractive on both sides and put lattice on it because he thinks his neighbor would appreciate it, and—don't frown at me like that, Sawyer, you know it's true!—I guess what I'm saying is, if we were friends, and if we were also having sex, I could get to like you a lot, more than would be good for either of us, because you're not available in that way. And I just think that would end up sucking for both of us and for the boys. So maybe let's just not go there?"

I set my jaw against the impulse to laugh—or kiss her. "But you're not saying *no*."

"Sawyer, *don't*."

I hold up a hand. "I won't try to talk you into anything."

She's right. I don't want anything serious. I know what

she's saying is true: it would be pretty easy for things to get out of control, being as we're in such close proximity to each other. There would have to be rules and regulations, something to keep it in line.

Then the answer occurs to me. "What about a one-time-only repeat?"

She looks intrigued at that. Or at least she doesn't immediately tell me to go to hell.

"What if we give Trevor and Helen something real to talk about?"

Her brows are drawn close together in confusion. "What do you mean?"

"When's the wedding?" I ask her.

She thinks about it a minute. "Three weeks—like a week and a half after school ends."

"Where?"

"Portland. Where Helen's from."

"So you have to get a hotel room."

"Yup."

"Is Madden going?"

She sighs. "This is a bone of contention between me and Trevor. I just think it's wrong. I mean, who doesn't invite their eight-year-old son to their wedding?"

I scrub my face irritably with my palm. "Do you think he researches all the ways to be a dick?"

She grimaces. "On the other hand, I'm sort of glad, you know? Because it would be so weird for me. To watch my son watch his father get married again. And it's a nighttime wedding, at a super-fancy location. So he's staying with my parents."

I am already picturing Elle dressed for a "super-fancy"

location, and liking the image it brings to mind. "So here's my thinking. Maybe we leave the boys with their respective grandparents, go to the wedding, and since Trevor thinks we're sleeping together anyway, for that one day—and night —we will be. But just that one day and night. Then we're done."

She bites into that plump lower lip. I work hard to resist the urge to bend over and lick the bitten spot. I will exercise restraint now to get what I want later.

"One time? Or one night?" she asks finally.

I take that as an excellent sign.

"Which do you want it to be?"

She thinks about that for a long time—another promising sign. Finally she says, "One time would be neater. But one night would be—" She eyes me, a head-to-toe appraisal. My dick stirs. Of course, he thinks it's all about him. And to be fair, her eyes do snag for a moment on my fly before her gaze comes up again to find mine. "One night maybe would be better for getting it out of our systems."

One night would definitely give me more time to work through the variations I pictured lying in bed that first night . . .

"One night it is," I say.

"But that's it. Once the night's over, nothing else."

I extend my hand and we shake on it.

18

ELLE

My phone buzzes.

Three weeks is a long time.

Sawyer.

If the phone had been pressed between my thighs when it vibrated, the message couldn't have taken a more direct path to my libido.

It's the last day of school before summer, and the boys are participating in their elementary school's "Moving Up" ceremony. We're sitting in the elementary school cafeteria-gymnasium, which is one of those battered-but-charming older school setups with pads on the walls, a low-slung stage, and beat-up folding chairs. The kids squirm in rows on the floor in front of the adults, and the whole room is steaming hot, despite a propped-open door in the back corner.

I'm overwhelmingly aware of Sawyer, three rows behind me. We drove separately and I hadn't thought to save him a seat. Actually, I'd thought about it, but it felt awkward to actually do it, because he and I aren't exactly friends, not yet. We exist in some weird in-between region. I've actually experienced something like this before, with other parents of kids Madden is friends with. You get to know kids' parents when you do drop-off and pickup from playdates, but you aren't quite officially friends with the parents on your own terms, where you'd invite them to socialize with you.

Plus with Sawyer and me there's this other complicating factor . . .

The one epitomized by the text on my screen, *Three weeks is a long time.*

Three weeks is *a long time,* I tap back. I don't bother, yet, to try to shield my phone screen, but I'm aware of the moms on either side of me, casting side-eye at my unruly device.

Sawyer's text is the first time either of us has mentioned his sex-repeat proposition since he laid it on the proverbial table Friday, after Trevor and Helen's awful visit. Sawyer finished the fence the next day, and since then, he's been—from my perspective—hiding out in his house and depriving me of my view. He hasn't even knocked on my door looking for Jonah. The boys have carried messages back and forth from house to house ("My dad says it's fine if I sleep over if it's fine with you."), but there have been no hot-dad visitations.

Which is as it should be. We made a deal. And honestly, I'm somewhat worried that if Sawyer starts making appearances on my doorstep, my resolve might not last long.

My phone vibrates, sending ripples up my legs. Or maybe that's just anticipation. *I have some ideas,* the text says.

Oh. I shift in my seat, suddenly aware of a strong desire to press my bare thighs together under my sundress.

I should ignore him. This isn't the time or the place. And the terms of our agreement stipulated only that one night.

And even if I'm thinking about violating that provision, I

should tell him we can resume this conversation later, when we're both in the privacy of our homes.

I text back, *Do tell.*

You look pretty in that dress.

Thank you.

You would look even prettier with that dress up around your waist.

I'm suddenly warm all over, with hot spots in certain key locations.

Are you going to wear a dress to the wedding?

Hattie and I are going shopping Saturday. Madden will be with my parents.

Yes.

I want to mess with you under the tablecloth.

Now I do press my thighs together—as subtly as possible. I think about how much better it would be if his hand were there, between my legs. Giving me something to shift and rub against. Finding the edge of my panties, creeping under the lace hem, sliding between my slick lips, parting me to rest a teasing fingertip against my swollen clit.

"There they go," whispers the woman next to me, and I wrench my attention back to where the third graders are edging forward on the floor to take the spot that had been occupied by the fourth graders. "They're so cute."

They are adorable, and I grab my phone and shove it unceremoniously into my purse, giving the kid spectacle my full attention. But I can't stop thinking about Sawyer's hand finding me under the table at the wedding reception.

I can't stop thinking about the fact that Sawyer is thinking about it.

The kids go back to their classrooms and the parents

file out. I stop to chat with several of Madden's classmates' parents, so it takes me a while to make my way out to the car. All the while, I'm hyperaware of my phone in my purse. I force myself to drive home, pull into the garage, and shut the door. Then I snatch the phone out of my purse like a starving woman lunging at an all-you-can-eat brunch.

There's a string of texts from Sawyer.

I'll behave myself in church.

Unless you don't want me to. I do have a lot of fantasies involving remote-control vibrators and church pews.

But once we're out of the church, all bets are off.

Oh, my. On both counts.

I'm going to make you come for the first time before we leave the reception.

I gasp.

Giving in to an impulse that's now almost an hour old, I slide my hand between my legs and cup myself where I'm damp and swollen. Lifting my hips to rub against my palm is irresistible, and the friction when I do makes me think I could make myself come in under a minute.

Instead, I text Sawyer back.

Not fair.

Right away, he texts back, *Oh, good, thought you'd gone dark on me.*

No, I just couldn't sext with the PTO looking over both my shoulders. Plus I was afraid of leaving a wet spot.

Were you?

The text is accompanied by an eggplant. I've never been much for either emojis or vegetables in a sexual context, but I have to admit, my desire to laugh is tempered by a swirl of arousal. I think it's because the visual reminds me of the way Sawyer fit—or barely fit—inside me.

I squeeze my hand tight between my thighs and wriggle.

Where are you now?

In my car. Still haven't made it into the house. Where are you?

In my workshop. I'm supposed to be finishing a table, but instead I'm imagining you on it.

Are you? I add a peach emoji, just for good measure.

What are you doing still in the car?

On a whim, I snap a selfie of my hand buried between my thighs.

Oh, Jesus. You trying to kill me?

The return photo is of flat abs, a jeans waistband, and a hand plunged deep behind the fly. My mouth goes dry.

What would it take to get you off? he texts.

Not much.

What if I told you what I'd do to you if I were there?

That would do it.

Put the phone down where you can see the screen.

I obey.

First thing is I'd get you naked because I didn't get to last time. And I think about it all the time, what you'd look like.

He thinks about me, naked, all the time? Does he mean that, or is that just a thing you say when you're trying to sext someone to orgasm?

I don't have time to think too long about it, because he keeps the goodness coming.

And then I'd taste you. Everywhere. I'd spend a long time on your mouth, but I want to bite your earlobes and lick your throat and kiss your collarbone, too. And I want to suck on your nipples until it's almost too much.

The combination of the fantasy he's evoking and the pressure of my hand is doing its work, fast. I'm panting and arching and wriggling, using my other hand to pinch and tweak my nipples.

But what I really want most is to lick between your legs.

A surge of heat and pure, sheer lust almost finishes me off.

"Hey Siri," I say. "Tell Sawyer Paulson I'm so close."

"Sending a text message to Sawyer Paulson that says 'I'm so close.'"

I want to get you so wet you can't tell what's you and what's me. Circle your clit, teasing you to the edge, and then pull back until you beg me to let you come.

With an involuntary cry, I come in fierce waves, bearing down on the armrest, digging my fingernails into the faux leather.

"Hey Siri. Tell Sawyer Paulson I just came."

"Sending a text message to Sawyer Paulson that says 'I just came.'"

A moment later:

Fuck, Elle. I'm right behind you.

And then:

Jesus. That was mega fucking good.

I laugh. And I return to my senses, amused and a little abashed by how thoroughly he made me lose my head. I'm sitting in my car with my dress hitched up and my hand between my legs, sexting my next-door neighbor. A neighbor who has already made me behave like a wild woman on another occasion and will quite likely make me do all kinds of things I won't respect myself for the next day at Trevor's wedding.

Wait. Speaking of Trevor's wedding . . .

I think that was technically cheating, I tell him.

Nah. It was foreplay.

Does that mean there could be other kinds of "foreplay" between now and our "one-time" repeat?

My still throbbing body gives that idea an enthusiastic thumbs-up.

19

ELLE

Hattie meets me at the Lucerne Mall on Saturday morning. She's wearing skinny jeans with a high waist, knee-high boots, and a cropped sweater that tapers to a wide band just above her waistline. Her black hair falls in glossy loose ringlets to her shoulders, and her makeup is impeccable.

Normally, I feel frumpy next to Hattie, who since her divorce has devoted an enormous amount of time to her appearance—Barrecore class, Pilates, regular cardio, time spent at Sephora and the Macy's makeup counter, hair, clothes, full-body waxing, you name it, she has pursued it in the interest of getting laid and moving on. I'm more the Ben-and-Jerry's-to-drown-your-sorrows type.

But today I'm feeling pretty darn good. I got up early enough to wash my hair and blow it dry, and I spent a long time doing my makeup and choosing my clothes.

I was thinking, *Who knows when I might need to send a selfie to a certain shameless next-door neighbor?*

"Wow," says Hattie. "You look fabulous."

"Thanks."

"Your dirty games with the neighbor obviously agree with you."

I'd told her the whole story, complete with Sawyer's rescuing me and my wounded pride from the Helen-and-Trevor-show, his kiss, the wedding-day proposition, and a very short expurgated version of the unexpected "foreplay" a few days ago. Hattie, being Hattie, had withheld judgment. She was delighted to hear I had a date to the wedding, that I was getting some, and that Trevor wouldn't "win."

"No dirty texts since the last day of school."

Which is fine. I've been checking my phone compulsively, of course, and have started flirty texts to Sawyer a few times, but I always delete them before sending. After what happened with Trevor—

I guess I want to be pursued, you know? I don't want to be the pathetic one ever again.

"Let's go make you irresistible," Hattie says.

Hattie is a great shopping assistant. We gather a pile of dresses in Nordstrom and she sends me into the dressing room.

The first two I don't even bother showing her. They're not good for my petite frame. Then come a few I need her advice about. She gives me a head shake, then another, then a lukewarm, "I don't hate that one . . ." Which makes us both laugh.

I've probably tried on ten dresses when I slip into one that unexpectedly makes me stop and catch my breath. I wouldn't have picked it off the rack, but Hattie has a good eye. Dusty pink isn't a color that looks good on most people, but this dress totally works for me. It falls to mid-calf, which is a length I usually loathe, but the tunic hemline is actually incredibly flattering. The sleeves are long, the cut simple and form-fitting with a choker neck, a low back, and a deep keyhole cutout that reveals a ton of cleavage without being cheap.

"Holy shit," Hattie says.

"I'll take that as a compliment," I say dryly.

"*I'd* fuck you," she says.

I laugh. "Sorry, get in line." I look back over my shoulder at my reflection in the mirror. "Should I take a picture and send it to Sawyer?"

She shakes her head. "No. You need to see his face the first time he sees you in that dress. But you should text him."

I hesitate a moment, but what the fuck.

Just bought a dress for the wedding.

I pocket my phone before I can get sucked into watching the three dots form . . .

The shoe department is next, where with Hattie's help, I find a pair of dusty-pink peep-toe kitten-heel sandals with three thin ankle straps. They make my legs look like I've been working out, and I can't stop admiring my calves in the mirror. It's been years since I wore heels.

"I don't get out enough," I tell Hattie.

"No, you don't."

"It's a good thing Sawyer doesn't want a relationship. I can practice on him and it won't matter that I'm rusty and lame."

"You're not rusty and lame," Hattie says.

"No, I know, I mean—but he can be my practice guy, and then I can date a lot and buy a lot of sexy clothes and shoes."

"With Trevor's money," Hattie adds. "You should keep a separate account with Trevor's alimony money and use it for all things you know would piss him off, like strappy sandals and vibrators and dates with other guys. Use your writing money and the child support for food and Madden's stuff and saving for college."

I laugh. "Do you do that?"

"If I ever actually received an alimony check I would do that," she says.

She doesn't talk much about her ex-husband. He was a jerk when they were married—borderline emotionally abusive and completely uninvested in her life or the kids—and now he barely sees the kids and is a complete deadbeat financially. To be fair, Trevor's rolling in money between his investment banking job and Helen's modeling work, but it isn't like Hattie's ex is broke, just a loser.

"How is the writing going, by the way?" Hattie asks.

"It's great," I say. "I think the fact that I'm willing to write pretty much anything has helped me out. I mean, I have the areas of focus and that helps me market—medical, scientific, tech—but I've been taking other work, copywriting, social media and blog content, whatever, and even without Trevor's money I think Madden and I would be fine."

Which is a great feeling, obviously. It's not PC to admit it, but I had a moment of sheer terror when Trevor said he was leaving. I had no idea whether I could make it on my own. He'd been supporting me for the last eight years, my writing jobs had dwindled to hobby level, and mixed in with all the hurt and anger was this thin, thready panic—*I can't be a single mom!*

But it turns out I can, and I'm pretty damn good at it.

"Have you done anything with the divorce book yet?"

"No."

"Come on, Elle, it's good! You should try to get it

published. Or get an agent. I have a friend who wrote a book about organizing your kitchen that wasn't one-eighth as cute or funny as your book and she wrote a proposal and sent it to an agent, and blammo! She's a bestseller."

"I don't think it usually works like that," I say dryly.

"Well, you won't know if you don't try, will you?"

"Guess not," I say, which I know is code for *I'm not planning to try,* but she can believe it means *You're right, Hattie! I should try!* if it'll let her sleep better at night.

I unstrap myself from the beautiful shoes. Midway, my phone buzzes, and I pull it from my pocket.

Picture or it didn't happen.

Hattie says I need to see your face the first time you see me in the dress.

I'm dying over here, Elle.

Wait till you see the shoes.

Hattie's face appears above my phone screen. "Quit sexting and let's go find something that'll really blow his mind."

At Victoria's Secret, Hattie and I take dressing rooms side by side.

"Oh, geez," she mutters. "I don't even know how to put this on." There's a rustle of clothing and then, "Yeah. No." More rustling. "That's more like it." She whistles softly. "Maybe that'll help. Elle. Can I confess something?"

"Sure."

"I have had some really bad sex in the last few months."

Laughter bursts out of me, and I think I hear someone laughing in the dressing room on the other side of me. It's so like Hattie to start this conversation in a semipublic place.

"I think men are watching too much porn," she laments. "I'm not a bicycle pump."

There's definitely laughter coming from the other dressing room. I'm biting back my own. "Hold that thought, Hattie. We'll discuss at lunch."

Meanwhile, I've donned a barely-there dusty-pink G-string and teeny-tiny lace demi-bra. And I'm staring at myself in the mirror, pleased with the result.

I grab my phone. *You're* really *going to like what I have on now.*

Tell me????

There is not very much of it. And it is pink. That is all I can say.

I hate you right now. Jonah is home and I can't even go upstairs and *imagine* for myself.

Maybe tonight?

Are you volunteering to help with the imagining?

I decide to leave him hanging—or, um, its opposite—for a bit on that question.

Do you play board games?

Standing in my workshop where the three coffee tables are almost done, I stare at my phone. That so wasn't the text I was hoping for. I'm still waiting for her to answer my question. The one about whether she was planning to help me out with my not-so-little problem, the erection I've been sporting on and off since she first texted me from the mall earlier today.

Or, let's face it, since I kissed her the other day.

I haven't spent this much time hard since I was thirteen, and I definitely haven't felt this frustrated. My right hand is not supplying the relief I desperately want, and if anything, my fantasies about the ways I want to kiss and touch and lick and fuck Elle Dunning are getting more vivid.

Not as a rule, I text back.

Madden and I just took out Settlers of Catan and we were wondering if you and Jonah wanted to play.

I don't know how.

We'll teach you.

If I'm being honest with myself, I will admit that my number-one motivation for agreeing to the invitation is that it will get me in the same room with Elle. Not that I think seeing her will in any way take the edge off my lust. But it's better than not seeing her.

Okay. Can we bring something? I have a pint of chocolate chip cookie dough ice cream in the freezer.

I never turn down chocolate chip cookie dough.

I immediately wonder how I can turn that knowledge to my advantage . . .

Then I start thinking about what it would be like to lick ice cream off her nipples . . .

It takes a while to cool down enough so I can head inside and convey the invitation to Jonah. He's thrilled, of course. While I run upstairs to change out of my work clothes, he grabs the ice cream from the freezer, then practically drags me out of our house, along the sidewalk, and up the steps to Elle and Madden's door.

Elle answers. She's wearing her sunny blond hair in a messy bun. She's cute and smiley, and she's one of those people who wears her happiness so close to the surface of the skin. She sort of vibrates with happiness, and I can't help smiling at her.

"I can't believe you've never played Catan!" she exclaims, throwing the door wide to let us in. "You're in for a treat."

After the texts we exchanged, part of my brain is stuck on the image of her in a fancy dress, so I have to adjust to the sight of a fitted white tank top and cropped yoga pants.

Not that it's an unhappy adjustment. Neither leaves anything to the imagination, and—yup. My dick hardens appreciably behind my fly, and I'm glad I'm wearing briefs and sturdy jeans.

I step inside, Jonah behind me, and we follow her into her dining room. I try not to glue my gaze to the curve of her ass under those skintight pants . . .

I force myself, instead, to notice my surroundings, which means her furniture. I tend to always look at other people's furniture with a critical eye, noticing where another craftsman cut corners or missed an opportunity to shine. Whoever made this table slathered way too much polyurethane on the surface, obscuring some beautiful quarter-sawn oak. I'd love to sand it down and redo it with an oiled finish, maybe replace the legs with something that would balance better with the weight of the top—these look too chunky.

Unlike Elle's legs. The yoga pants cling to her thighs, which are that perfect combination of strong and soft, and come to an enticing vee where I want to bury my face.

I jerk my attention back to the contents of the room, a much safer subject. Her dining room window faces my house. I step to the window and look out. The fence looks pretty good from here; I'm pleased with my work, though I make a mental note that she's more or less looking straight down on it. I'll check, tomorrow, to make sure it looks as good as I want from the top.

"That's the window I stalk you through," she blurts.

I turn back to discover her with her hand clapped over her mouth. She's bright red.

"Stuff just falls out when I open my mouth," she whispers, dropping her hand.

Which of course makes me look at her mouth. She is

wearing pale pink sparkly gloss, and I imagine she would taste like raspberry if I licked her.

She would taste like Elle, if I licked her.

Jonah and Madden are hunched over a rectangular box on the table, removing tons and tons of little fiddly pieces and fully engaged in the process, so I take a step toward her and say, "I like it."

She bites her lip. "My mouth?"

"Mmm-hmm. And the things that fall out of it, too." I lean close and brush her ear with my breath. "There are also some things I would like to put in it. My tongue, for starters."

"Oh," she says. Really, more like "ohhh," but it's quiet enough not to attract the attention of the boys, who are busily constructing a complicated board out of a series of hexagonal pieces.

"You sit here," Madden says, pointing me to my seat, "and you sit here, Mom, and Jonah, you're here."

I'm not sure what I'm expecting, but I actually really like the game. It's complex enough to be interesting and simple enough not to make my brain hurt. There's lot of interaction and a bit of screw-your-buddy, and before long Elle and I are locked in a tight contest for first place. She takes the "longest road" card, and then I steal it back, but she quickly retaliates by grabbing the "largest army" card. We both have nine victory points and need only one to win. And—wouldn't you know it—we're competing over a single intersection. Whoever gets the resources he or she needs to build a settlement there is going to win.

It's my turn. And all I need is to convince someone to trade me a forest hex resource—lumber—and I'll have what I need to win. I try Madden first, but he doesn't have one, and then I try Jonah, but he doesn't have one, and then I turn to Elle and say, "I don't suppose you have any wood you'd give me," and she gives me this thousand-watt seductive smile and mouths, "Isn't that my line?"

Then, while I'm still trying to find a single functioning brain cell, she asks the boys, "How dumb does he think I am? If I give him my wood, he'll win."

Not dumb at all. Smart as a whip, fun to be around, and really fucking pretty, with wisps of her blond hair tumbling out of the messy bun and her mouth all glossy and that sheen of happy coming off her skin.

And I realize:

I'm not at all unhappy to let her win this game, except that it means the night's over and Jonah and I have to go back to our side of the fence.

21

ELLE

"You can't go," Madden informs Sawyer and Jonah. "We haven't had ice cream."

Thank God for small boys and their ironclad memory for dessert, because I don't want this evening to be over.

Playing Catan with Sawyer is six thousand times more fun than playing with Trevor ever was. Trevor is a grudging game player, fussy and nervous, and doesn't have a competitive bone in his body.

Sawyer plays Catan exactly perfectly—like it matters more than anything and couldn't matter less. I'm not sure how to explain it, but anyone who loves games knows what I'm talking about. In order for them to be fun, you have to invest yourself fully and you also have to not take yourself too seriously.

Maybe that's true of other things, too, like sex and relationships and life itself, and that's why I find it to be such an attractive trait.

Not that anything other than sex is on the table here.

"No, we can't go before ice cream," Sawyer says, and his eyes catch mine, and he's smiling. Really smiling, not just the tipped-up cautious Sawyer smile that I am used to, and I swear, it almost breaks me. I want to tell him, *You absolutely cannot smile like that in my presence if you want me to be able to do this sex thing with you without crossing the line and falling for you and all the things that neither of us wants to have happen.*

I serve up four generous bowls of ice cream (the boys think it's Christmas in June) and we sit back down at the dining room table and eat in near silent ice-cream bliss.

"Do you pick the cookie dough out, or eat everything together?" I poll them.

"All together," Sawyer says, digging in with a gusto that reminds me, pleasurably, of how he does certain other things.

"I pick the cookie dough out and eat that first, then the ice cream," Jonah says.

"Me, too," Madden says.

I take a dainty spoonful of all-vanilla. "I eat the ice cream first and leave the cookie dough for last."

They all look at me like I'm crazy.

I shrug. "I like to have something to look forward to."

"Do you have something you're looking forward to right now?" Sawyer asks, so innocently that for a split second I don't make the connection that he's messing with me. Then I catch the look on his face and feel that glorious tugging sensation in my low belly right down to my core.

I can't really answer his question, because it's not fair for me to say in front of Madden how much I'm looking forward to his dad's wedding that he's not invited to, or to getting to sightsee in Portland while I'm there, so instead I say, "I do, actually," and match Sawyer's dark-eyed look with my own.

I'm rewarded with a faint bloom of color across his cheekbones. I wonder where else blood is moving, and that thought brings a sweep of heat down my body. For reasons that I can't completely explain, I put on one of the bra-and-panty sets I bought today before Sawyer and Jonah came over. I wasn't actually thinking there would be an opportunity to show it off, so I guess in a way it was just for me. Just so I'd know. And indeed, I'm hyperconscious of the thin strip of lace barely covering my swollen lips.

"Anyone want more ice cream?"

"I'll take another small spoonful," Sawyer says.

"Me too!" two other voices chime in.

"Give me your bowls. I'll get it."

I take the bowls into the kitchen, drag the ice cream out of the freezer, and pull out my phone.

I'm wearing some of my new purchases. Unfortunately, the panties have suffered a little bit of a—setback. They're such a thin scrap to begin with, not much absorption potential . . .

I can hear Sawyer's phone buzz in the next room. I scoop ice cream and wait patiently.

You are evil, woman.

You were the one who started the "foreplay."

"Mom! Can Jonah sleep over?"

I carry the ice-cream bowls back into the dining room. Sawyer's eye catches mine. This is a parental moment, not the other kind, but I still register the buzz of intentional eye contact, and I smile involuntarily at him. He smiles back, and shrugs, as if to say, *Okay with me.*

"Sure," I say.

We finish up our ice cream, and it's nine thirty now, well

past the boys' weekend bedtime, so we need to move the party along. "Boys, pjs and teeth."

The boys rush off. Jonah won't need to get sleepover stuff from his house, because his stuff has gradually migrated over here. I have a pair of his pajamas that go through the wash with Madden's, and his extra toothbrush and toothpaste live in our bathroom drawer.

"I'll help you clean up," Sawyer says.

We'd pushed all the Catan bits into the middle of the table to eat ice cream, but now he leans across the table and begins bagging up all the little wooden pieces. I work on collecting the cards. "It's a really good game," he says. "I'm not a game guy, but I actually liked this one. I haven't played a board game since—"

He goes suddenly silent.

Right.

"—since Lucy died," he finishes—because we both knew that was what he was going to say; there's no use pretending it wasn't. He shoots me an apologetic look.

"It's okay," I say, meaning it. Or at least really wanting to mean it. There's a sore spot in my chest, because Sawyer's so great, and it must have been lovely to be Lucy, to be the woman he talked about like the sun rose and set wherever she was. "You gotta be able to talk about her, right? And look at me, I'm the one blathering about my divorce when I'm trying to hook up with a stranger in a bar. Look," I say. "You've been more than clear about what you want out of this, where you stand, all that, and I'm a big girl. So—let's just be who we are, shall we? Battered and maybe in need of some TLC, and by no means ready to shake off the past and march undaunted into the future. It doesn't mean we can't have a little fun."

He stares at me for a long moment, and I can't figure out what he's thinking. Then he says, "Are you sure?"

"'Course I'm sure."

"You're a good sport."

"Why, thanks," I say, and his praise is nice, but I feel a flutter of regret, like seller's remorse. Though I don't know exactly what it is I think I've given up. Nothing I ever had to begin with.

We finish dumping the pieces into the sturdy Catan box, and I pull the cover back on. He rises from the table and shifts his weight from one foot to the other. I'm sure he's about to tell me he has to go, has to get back to the house for whatever reason, but instead he sits down suddenly and says, "Hey. How about a rematch?"

22

SAWYER

I'm merciless. And she loves it.

I'm talking about the board game, folks—eyes up here.

I beat her ten victory points to eight. We're so involved in wiping each other across the land of Catan that we forget to check on the boys, but when we finish playing and go downstairs, we discover them sound asleep on their side-by-side sleeping bags.

I bend down, smooth Jonah's hair, and kiss the top of his head. Beside me, I feel Elle crouch, whispering *I love you* to Madden, kissing his cheek. When she stands, our eyes snag across the sea of nylon, artificial down, and small boy, and we share a smile. It is a smile that says this single-parenting thing is really hard and totally worth it.

I follow her upstairs. Really, it's just another excuse to watch her muscles and the other awesomeness that is Elle move under that stretchy fabric. Apparently I am a weak man, because as she reaches the top step, I reach out and touch. Just a quick swipe of my hand over the sweet curve of her ass, but my badly behaved fingers squeeze.

We reach the top step just then; she steps into the kitchen and turns to face me, and my hand, which seems unwilling to let go of its handful of flesh, tugs her tight up against me.

She makes a sound, a gasp, a moan, I don't know—I just know it goes straight to my dick, which is already ragingly hard at the feel of her through briefs and jeans and the absurdly thin fabric of those wretched pants. I yank her closer (as if there's such a thing) and my mouth finds hers fiercely, aggressively—I would be worried I was hurting her except she's whimpering and clutching at me and whispering my name.

She kicks the downstairs door closed and I push her up against it—vertical seems to be our jam—and we kiss and kiss, tongues grappling and teasing, hands roving.

I grab her tank top and pull it up because if I don't get my mouth on her nipples in the next three seconds—

I don't know. There is no end to that sentence. It's an imperative.

She is wearing a white bra that barely covers her nipples and is trimmed with a thin rim of lace. I want to dive in, but I want to savor what I see more. The lush abundance—her breasts are gorgeously full for such a petite woman—the pale pink nipples, the dusky pink disks that frame them. I nuzzle a curve, lick her areola, circle in and find her nipple so tight against my tongue that both of us gasp. I tease her, matching my tongue on this side with my fingers on the other, and she arches her back and pushes into my face, all that smooth flesh right there for the tasting.

I slide my hand down the flat of her stomach to the waist-band of her yoga pants, breach the elastic and linger there, teasing my fingertips across the soft flesh of her lower belly.

She tips her pelvis up toward my fingers, asking for more, which makes my dick surge forward in anticipation.

"Foreplay," I remind her, but really I'm reminding myself. We're not going to have sex tonight, no matter how much I want to.

That doesn't mean we can't do lots of other things.

Running the risk that interrupting the flow here means she'll come to her senses and kick me out, I say, "Can we—should we? Go upstairs? Is there a lock on your door?"

She hesitates.

"No sex," I say, as my body tries to argue exactly the opposite. But this is what separates men from beasts—we get to overrule our dicks. "Not till the wedding."

She bursts out laughing, and it takes me a moment to hear what I've said.

"Trevor's wedding," I clarify, grinning. "No sex till then, but that doesn't mean I can't make you feel good. I want to make you feel really good."

"I can get behind that," she says, with a groan, tugging her bra up and shirt down. "Jesus, Sawyer, I really thought you were going to get me off without even touching my clit."

My turn to groan. "Can you say that whole sentence again?" I'm exceptionally glad to note that her propensity to say whatever comes into her head applies to sex, too. I may not talk much myself, but dirty-wise I am a guy who appreciates talk, the more the merrier.

Instead she grabs my hand and leads me up the stairs. I

realize that her house's layout is a mirror image of mine, just as she turns into a bedroom and flips on a light.

The decor is dark—mostly forest green and cream, a green rug, thick drapes, and a quilt with overlapping fern patterns. I hate it immediately.

"It was Trevor's taste." She bites her lip and gives me a chagrined look, like the one I gave her after I inadvertently blurted out that I hadn't played a board game since Lucy died. I think both of us would like to forget for a while about the other two people in the room and just enjoy each other. So I decide that's what's going to happen. I pick her up and, tickling her, deposit her on the bed and throw myself down next to her, and then, before either of us can think, I kiss her.

Kissing her lying down is a whole new level of insane. I climb over her and settle my weight on my elbows; she spreads her legs and invites me to tuck my hips—including my voracious denim-clad erection—between. God, it's good, the pressure, the heat of her, the squeeze of her thighs around my legs, the sound she makes when I wiggle, barely enough to count as movement, against her.

"That feels so good," she whispers, wiggling back.

I slow us down so we can both worship the way it feels to kiss like this—the nibble of her mouth at my lips, the stroke of her tongue against mine, the heat and wetness, the give and take, the sounds in my chest and in the back of her throat. I could do this all night, but I don't think she'd let me. Because mixed into the sweetness and the softness, the tug and slip and slick, I feel her teeth and fingernails and another wiggle, this one clearly of frustration, against me.

I turn onto my side and slide my hand up her tank top. I

spread my fingers across the expanse of soft skin, I tug at the half-cups of her bra, I tweak those nipples until she says, "Fuck you, Sawyer, you're a pussy-tease."

Yes. I knew she'd be like this the first night we fucked, even though I don't think she said a word while I was inside her. Still, somehow I knew she would be rude and dirty and excellent in exactly this way.

So obligingly, I slide my hand into her pants, part her lips, with their soft curls, slick her wetness all over her, but especially around her clit, circling.

"You gotta tell me, baby," I say. "I'll give you choices, but you gotta tell me."

She whimpers.

I make the smallest circles I can, teasing the innermost bud.

"Mmm-hmm," she hums.

I widen the circle a little, letting the hood and inner lips cover her so it's not so intense.

"Yes!" she cries.

My hand slides lower on a sweet slick of her wetness, my fingers finding her wet heat, probing, entering, thrusting.

"God, Sawyer, yes."

"Which?"

"All—of—the—above—"

"I should have known."

I stop for just long enough to push her shirt up and her bra down, giving me access to her breasts, to her beaded nipples; I take one in my mouth and send my hand back down her pants. I fuck her with my fingers until she's fucking back, and then, with my thumb, I make big gentle circles, spiraling in tighter and tighter until all I have to do is tap her bare clit—

And then I get what I've been working for, a low, muddy murmur of: "Sawyer please, Sawyer, yes, please, oh my God, oh my God, just like that, Sawyer, Sawyer, Sawyer, Sawyer, SawYER!"

23

ELLE

"Can I help you with that?"

I've roused myself from my post-orgasmic stupor. I've been lying in a blissful daze beside Sawyer, not moving, not thinking, but a moment ago my blurred brain registered the slow crawl of his hand back and forth over the bulge in his jeans.

"You must be dying," I say, reaching for the button of his fly.

"Nah," he says gallantly.

"Seriously, Sawyer, I am all for everyone getting off, you know?"

"I won't fight you," he says, releasing a frustrated exhalation, and making me laugh.

He helps me with the button and zipper of his jeans—no mean feat with his erection fighting back at us. I finally free him from his jeans and briefs and hold him in my hand, hot, hard, and incredibly satisfying. When we fucked in the alley outside the bar, I didn't get to see him or touch him with my hand, so this feels all new. I love the velvet softness of the skin, taut and smooth over the swollen head. Penises are the best, and this is quite possibly the best of all penises.

"Why thank you," Sawyer says, the first hint that I've spoken aloud. That happens to me from time to time; I think something is in my head and it turns out I've said it aloud. Usually it's not quite as dirty as this, though.

"I don't have a huge basis for comparison," I say, sliding down the bed so I can lick a teardrop of pre-cum off him. And then I pop the whole head into my mouth, because, hey, I'm here, and, best of all penises.

He groans his approval and I feel the throb of blood under my tongue, which only eggs me on. I pull back and start again so I can lick him thoroughly and systematically, and so I can tease him, first the slit, then circles around it, then the whole head, then, pop, in my mouth again, sliding him against the softness of my cheek. I work my mouth down him bit by bit, licking him, licking my lips, getting us both wet and lubed up, making room for him deeper and deeper until I feel him against the back of my throat and hum in welcome.

"Jesus, Elle," he says. "You look like such a little blond angel and you are so unbelievably badass."

It's funny, though (I think, not pausing in lavishing affection on the best of all penises), but I'm not. I never have been, anyway. Sawyer has brought out a side of me I didn't know I had. Or maybe I suspected, briefly, at the beginning of things with Trevor, but then Trevor made it clear in a variety of kind, subtle ways that he wasn't much for my dirty streak, so it went underground, and I didn't think I missed it. I didn't think it mattered.

My natural naughtiness is incredibly happy to be on display again.

I bob my head up and down, angling myself so I can take more of him, letting him thrust a little against my throat before I nudge his hips to let him know how much I can take —and he's good; he backs off right away, so we get into this rhythm of him pushing and me pushing back. He's talking now, quietly, telling me how good it feels, how good I am, how hot I am, and he reaches down to find both my nipples and tweaks them gently, which somehow makes me able to take more.

"Elle, if you don't want me to come in your mouth—" he says, but I shake my head and tug his hips toward me and circle him, hard, fierce, with my tongue, drawing a pattern like an infinity symbol up the shaft and around the velvet curve of the head, and he trembles all over with the effort of holding himself back and comes, shaking, rigid, murmuring my name.

"Wow," he says. "Wow. Wow."

I giggle.

I slide my hand down between my legs and touch the wetness there. There's a lot more than before. He watches me do it. "You like that," he says wonderingly.

"Yeah," I say.

I realize what he's not saying. Lucy didn't used to.

Well.

I won't let myself think anything other than, *Interesting.*

24

SAWYER

I'm on my hands and knees, pounding—

We've been through this before, haven't we? You all have dirty minds. I'm installing a hardwood floor.

Some guys like to use staples. I prefer the old-fashioned nails.

In the end, I did go for salvaging my own boards—I heard through the woodworkers' grapevine, which is mostly centered out of that Seattle reclaimed lumberyard I mentioned, that there was an old church being torn down and that the flooring was up for grabs. I pulled Brooks in, and Brooks pulled Chase and Jack in, and Jack pulled his friend Henry in, and before I knew it, the five of us were loading our trucks and dumping hardwood at my house.

Since then I've been recutting tongue-and-groove where necessary, cutting board lengths, laying floor, and hammering nails.

Which is an excellent outlet for all my frustrations.

I didn't realize how difficult a challenge I was setting for both Elle and me when I declared that we wouldn't have sex until Trevor's wedding. I haven't been this sexually on edge since I was fifteen and Cindy McNamara and I were doing everything-but on a regular basis. Grown men (or at least this grown man) aren't accustomed to this kind of waiting game, particularly if the other party is also a ready, willing, able, and enthusiastic participant.

I have thought several times about just abandoning all pretense, showing up at Elle's house with condoms in hand, and getting this out of our systems. There's a vivid set of fantasies to go with that plan, mostly involving what it would feel like to kiss her and fuck her at the same time, so the slick of tongue and squeeze of pussy blend together in my muzzy head into one hot, wet mess.

The thing that keeps me from doing it—breaking the rules—is the knowledge that the pretense is what's keeping both of us from freaking out. As brave a face as Elle puts on, as strong and competent as she comes across, I'm not sure she's ready to tackle something like a relationship. And I know I'm not. This wacky game we're playing lets us have at each other without needing to explain, define, or analyze it.

And that's a good thing.

Jonah and Madden bound through the front door and into the living room.

"Can we help?" Madden asks, watching me with a wide, admiring gaze. It feels nice to be hero-worshipped from time to time. I'm guessing Madden, in particular, doesn't have much experience with carpentry, since Mr. Yap doesn't seem like the type to do it himself.

I eye the two of them, light and dark, assessing their ability not to smash their fingers. "Sure." I show them where I need the nails to go, and set them up with two smaller hammers. I know they'll lose interest in a few minutes, and that's okay, but it's not a bad thing to get some experience with stuff early on—practice definitely makes perfect.

Sure enough, after each of them has put three or four nails into the wood (several getting bent in the process, but that's okay), they bounce up and declare themselves done. They're going to go looking for salmonberries in the bushes behind our houses.

I don't try to talk them into staying. When Jonah gets a little older, I will offer to teach him more, but for now I'm content to give him a taste. I'm not naive enough to think that because I love woodwork, he will. I do think, with great warmth and affection, of the days I spent learning carpentry at my dad's side, but I know nothing ruins good memories faster than trying to recapture them. Anyway, for now these boys need to be outside, playing and exploring, enjoying these early days of summer.

"Hey," I ask. "Whatever happened with Mr. Ketotzi and Junie?" I realize that with all the things in my head—Elle's compact, sexy body not the least—I let the school year end without ever checking back in.

They look at me like I'm speaking a foreign language, which I probably am. Let's face it, once school's out, it's like it never happened. Madden seems to be looking a long way into the distance, or possibly inside his own head; I'm not sure which. "He apologized to Junie in front of the class," Madden says. "And he said that from now on Junie—and all of us—could line up or be chosen for teams or whatever, however we wanted to be. And he apologized to Jonah and me for saying we were girls, unless we wanted to be girls."

I can hear the grudging note in the whole apology from a

thousand miles away, but I still appreciate how things turned out, that Mr. McKibben laid it all out for Mr. Ketotzi and that Mr. Ketotzi, however under duress he must have been, did the right thing. And most of all, how the boys forced the adults to look at themselves in the mirror.

"You did good," I tell the boys. "You did a good job. That must feel good."

Madden nods, a compact nod that hints at the way he'll be as a teenager and as a man, too cool for a big emotional show.

I watch them as they go. If Madden's too cool, I'm not—I'll admit it. My chest feels tight.

I pull out my phone.

Madden's a great kid. I'm glad he's in my kid's life.

Her reply comes back quickly.

Right back atcha in reverse. Love that they look out for each other.

And everyone else, too, apparently.

It's only as I grab a handful of nails and resume pounding that I realize I forgot to wish I could tell Lucy.

25

ELLE

I t's been several nights since Sawyer and I played Catan and then retreated to my bedroom. Every time I replay the events of that evening, I find myself smiling. And then frowning, because I don't quite know what to make of the whole thing. I mean, I know what to make of the oral sex —it was terrific, in both directions. But the other parts, the parts that were cozy and friendly and almost family-ish, the text he sent me the day after about Madden being a good kid . . .

Those parts scare the shit out of me. I think I might need to back away from that kind of stuff, the hanging out and playing games and almost—almost co-parenting. Because I could get to like it, and I don't think that matches Sawyer's expectations. Plus, there's the promise I made myself: no more falling for guys who are in love with someone else.

Luckily, over the next few days, things swing back toward the pure-sex side. Sawyer and I text each other a bunch of times. At first it's in the vein of, um, reminiscences. As in:

Him: *I get hard again every time I think about what you did to me last night.*

Me: *Me too. I mean, not hard. Wet. You know what I mean.*

And it plunges into the gutters from there.

Him: *Jonah's asleep.*

Me: *Madden, too.*

Him: *Call me and I'll talk you off.*

Me: *Is that a thing?*

Him: *Phone sex?*

Me: *I've just never heard the phrase "talk you off."*

And my phone rings.

"Let me demonstrate," he says. "What do you do? When you're by yourself?"

"I, uh—pretty much what you did the other night, minus the fingering. I just can't coordinate all that action."

"You mean I offer value-add?" he suggests smirkily.

I smile. "I guess you do, kind of."

"Well, let me add some value. You do the circles and I'll do the dirty talk about my dick and your pussy."

I groan.

"Is that a yes?"

"That's a yes."

Once he's accomplished his task, I offer to reciprocate.

"Are you, like, a fist guy? Or—I know guys who fuck the mattress."

"You have such a filthy mouth, Elle, and I love it so hard."

Hearing the word *love* come out of his mouth throws me for a momentary loop, but I get a hold on myself. "Thanks."

"More of a fist guy. And I love myself some lube. The more the merrier. Soap, saliva, the bottled stuff, whatever."

"Okay. Do that. Whichever. Your favorite."

I actually hear the click of the lube cap through the phone.

"But imagine it's me. I mean, my lube. Like, imagine your hand is my pussy and the slippery stuff is me, wanting you really bad. I've got plenty of it here for you, by the way."

"Oh. Oh, wow."

"Are you lying on your back?"

"Mmm-hmm."

He's already breathless, which makes me feel pretty damn good about my talking-off technique.

"So then I guess I'm riding you. Sinking down on you, pulling back almost all the way off so you can feel me all along your length. Then hard and fast. Which is better?"

"They're both good. God, you're getting me there so fast."

"Go for it."

"I am."

"Do you want me to lie down on you so we can kiss? Or sit up so you can watch me jiggle?"

"Jesus, Elle, where'd you get that imagination?" His voice is wound to the breaking point, which makes my pussy thrum.

I don't tell him I'm not usually this bold, that he makes me want to say and do wild stuff like this. It feels too clingy, too relationship-y. Not the right vibe for two people who have agreed that all of this is just foreplay for a single main event. I just say, "Which one, stud?"

"Jiggle," he says, but the word dissolves in his mouth into a groan and then my name, in a short, harsh cry.

"Okay, then," I say, laughing. "I know how to get you off fast at Trevor's wedding."

He doesn't say anything for what feels like several

minutes. Then he says, "I made a mess. I'll be right back. Washcloth time."

When he comes back from cleaning up and picks up his phone, he says, "You want to cuddle? Have a cigarette?"

I laugh.

"Nah, I'm serious. We can hang up. Or we can, you know, hang out."

"Hang out, I guess," I say. I'm surprised that he asked it, and surprised how much I want to.

We chat for a while about nothing in particular. How he got started with furniture making (he learned a lot of stuff from his dad, who was a general contractor in the Oregon town where he grew up, but then he took woodworking in high school and realized he wanted to build furniture, not be a GC), his relationship with his brother (they beat the snot out of each other as kids and still give each other a hard time, but they love each other). Then we switch to me: When I started writing (for my elementary school newsletter), how it feels to be an only child (I used to love getting all the attention, but now that I'm grown, I feel like I missed out on an experience—plus I worry about not having anyone to help me take care of my parents when they get old). I tell him my parents live in the foothills of the Cascades but have been talking about moving closer to Seattle to be nearer to me and Madden. My mom's a therapist and my dad's a mutual fund manager.

"They're pretty good parents."

"Are they happy together?"

"They're still married."

I think they're happy together. They're cute together, anyway, finishing each other's sentences, my dad the type to still open doors and pull out chairs for my mom. I guess you never know, though, do you?

As if he can read my mind, he asks, "How did you meet Trevor?"

"It's a sad story. Are you sure you want to hear it?"

"I think I can take it," he says dryly.

I'd temporarily forgotten that he has a whole new dimension on sad; nothing I can tell him can possibly touch the grief he's experienced.

"A dog got hit by a car, and its owner, a teenaged kid, found it, and didn't know what to do—he was distraught, standing over the body, crying, his hands shaking so bad he couldn't even text his mom. Trevor was walking from one direction and I was walking from the other, and we stopped to help. I had a blanket in my car a block away, and we wrapped the dog up and carried it back to the teenager's house, where his mom was. The whole thing was awful. But then Trevor said we should go out for a drink, so we did. And he was so great about the whole thing—stopping, being totally in control about the emergency situation, super calm —and then afterward, so sweet to me. I fell hard for him. I didn't know until a little bit later that he'd just gotten viciously dumped, and that he was rebounding and I was in the wrong place at the wrong time." I draw a deep breath. I'm tucked into bed, warm and comfortable and bonelessly relaxed, and the memory still has all its old resonances—the sadness of the dog's death and the bright promise of meeting someone wonderful—only now it's all overwritten with Trevor's betrayal. "Maybe a dead dog isn't an auspicious meeting? I should have known."

Sawyer snorts.

I toy with the edge of my sheet, wondering if I should ask him about his wife. It feels weird to tell him about Trevor and not ask him anything about his marriage.

"How'd you meet Lucy?"

I can hear his indrawn breath. I remember all too vividly how he shut down the last time I brought her up. "You don't have to tell me."

"I don't mind. You told me about Trevor. She owned a store, a high-end craft design boutique. And she saw my furniture, and she wanted to stock it. I brought her a few pieces, and—well, one thing led to another."

My stomach clenches. So she'd been not only his wife but his patron and his partner. I remind myself that I'm not trying to compete with her or take her place, and I feel a sharp wave of relief, the perfect reminder not to get in too deep. "What happened to the store?"

"We—we closed it after she died. None of us—her parents, her sisters, me—were passionate about it the way she was. But it hurt to do it. When she knew she was dying, she told me flat out that she didn't want anyone keeping it open to honor her, only if we genuinely wanted to run it, but —I still feel crappy about it."

"I'm sure she would understand."

He goes silent on the other end of the phone, and I feel like I've overstepped, that presuming to know anything about how his late wife would feel is too much, especially in this situation we're in. Then he says, "I think she would've liked you."

That makes me smile. Warmth spreads in my chest, sending flares out in all directions.

Danger, Will Robinson! Danger!

"Um, thanks." I take a deep breath. "I, um, I should go."

It comes out more abrupt than I mean it to.

"Yeah, okay," he says easily. "Well, nice cuddling with you."

"Ditto."

After I hang up, I lie in bed, wondering what's happening. How I feel. If he feels it too. What it means.

What kind of a glutton for punishment I am.

It takes me a long, long time to fall asleep.

26

SAWYER

Two days before Jonah's ninth birthday, I realize I've screwed up.

Jonah invited Madden and eight other boys to go bowling at the local alley, then back to the house afterward. Jonah's grandparents will be there, serving pizza and lighting candles on an ice-cream cake. We'll open presents and maybe let the boys run around in the backyard.

It was my idea, and Jonah loved it. He danced around the living room, he was so excited, and as the party gets closer, he's bubbling with anticipation. I've been feeling like a superstar—except I just realized that I've invited nine boys to come back to my house after bowling, and I have no way to transport them all. The grandparents are doing party setup and pizza and cake acquisition, and anyway, one set drives a Mini and the other a Fiat. Short of asking all their parents to come back out halfway through the party to drive them, I'm stuck.

When I realize my mistake, I'm frustrated and angry at myself, but mostly?

I'm sad.

Because Lucy wouldn't have screwed this up. She would have been all over the logistics from minute one. She'd have lists and notes, and she'd buzz from room to room, asking Jonah's opinion about things and picking up the phone and dashing off emails until everything was ironclad. She'd organize all the other moms into a driving machine—

Other moms.

Right.

I'm still not good at the inter-mom-schmooze-fest, and I suck at things like setting up carpools, but there's one mom who I know will come to my rescue. And who I won't feel weird about asking.

I grab my phone and dash off a text to Elle.

Hey. Are you there? Can I come ask you something?

The three dots appear. How much human productivity do you think has already been lost to watching those three dots wiggle, waiting for an answer?

A minute later, her answer pops up.

I'm here but have a phone interview in twenty minutes so if this is a booty call—

My mind had been elsewhere, but as soon as she says *booty call,* it starts wandering a different path, taking some key portions of my anatomy with it. I almost text back to reassure her I can make both of us very happy in twenty minutes —but I have a real problem to solve here. I squelch the fantasy, give my dick a stern talking-to, and jog over to her house, my hard-on subsiding just in time for my arrival. She opens the door before I can knock, stepping out onto the front stoop and shutting the door behind her.

"Are you worried that if you let me into the house you won't be able to keep me out of the bedroom?" I tease, my best intentions vanishing instantly upon seeing her. She's wearing skinny jeans, knee-high boots, and a tight black T-shirt. I have an immediate vision of peeling her—because that's what it would take—out of her clothing.

"I'm serious, Sawyer—keep it clean."

"You're the one whose mind obviously went to the worst, dirtiest place the second you saw my text."

She presses her lips together to hide a smile, then—unintentionally, I think—licks them.

Aaaand I'm hard again.

Concentrate, Paulson.

"This is a big ask, but is there any way you'd be willing to play chauffeur for the party on Saturday? I just realized I screwed up and I have no way to get the boys back here after bowling. If I'd thought it through, I could have done the whole party package, but I was being cheap and I didn't want all the grandparents to have to schlep out there."

She smiles. "Not cheap. Sensible. Those party packages are insanely overpriced. And it's nice of you to think about the grandparents. So you want me, what, to just show up with the van at the end of the bowling, and load up half of them?"

"I—guess so?" But now that she says it, it sounds kind of mercenary. "Why don't you come bowling with us? I should have invited you to begin with. It would be great to have another adult, and Jonah likes you."

Her expression tightens. And I hear my own words a second later.

Nice job, Paulson.

I take a deep breath. "It would be great—for me—to have you there."

A smile teases around the corners of her mouth. She's so

freaking pretty when she smiles. I reach out and touch her cheek, soft as satin.

She draws back, wagging a finger. "None of that." She tilts her head. "Yes. I would be happy to do the driving, and I would be honored to be included in the birthday festivities."

"And—no pressure—pizza and cake afterward. If you don't mind two sets of grandparents."

I think better of it as soon as the words are out of my mouth. Lucy's parents will probably get emotional at some point, and I don't want to subject Elle to that.

But it's too late to retract the invitation now, and Elle seems like she can handle it. She's pretty unflappable.

"I'm used to grandparents," she says dryly. "They can't be any more horrifying than Trevor's parents."

"Apple doesn't fall far from the tree?" I wager.

She grimaces and shakes her head. "You got that right. Speaking of signs I should have heeded."

"I guess I'll get to meet them, or at least admire them from a distance, at Trevor's wedding."

"Lucky you," she says, rolling her eyes and peeking at her watch.

"You have a few more minutes." I raise one eyebrow and let my gaze drop down over her skin-hugging outfit.

She twists one hand in the other uneasily. "I like to be sitting in my chair, fingers on the keys, ready to dial, a few minutes before the actual appointed time of the interview. So I can, you know, clear my head."

I can't ignore a red flag waved in my face like that. Before she can react, I bend to kiss her, deep and thorough.

She moans into my mouth.

I let her go, and she takes an uneven step back against her

front door. Her mouth is open, her lower lip is soft and wet, and her eyes are glazed with desire.

I want to do it again, but I'll have to be satisfied with my work—for now.

"Now you really need to go clear your head."

"I hate you," she says, but she's smiling all out, and what the hell, I grab her and kiss her once more for good measure before I trot back to my house.

I whistle as I walk.

27

ELLE

Eight-year-old boys in a bowling alley are like an unconfined litter of twelve-week-old puppies. They boil and bubble around and over each other, they race off before you can stop them to God knows where, they are fearless and dopey, totally lovable and totally terrifying.

It's a good thing I came along, because even under ideal circumstances this isn't a one-parent job.

We bowl in two adjacent lanes. Sawyer and I each take a lane and five boys. Madden and Jonah told us ahead of time they wanted to be together, so I read off two lists of boys' names so the boys won't fight about who goes where. I take Madden and Jonah and three other boys, Griggs, Emmett, and Caden. The boys immediately begin fighting about turn order and bragging about their past bowling exploits.

Once we've got their names entered into the bowling computers and the gutter guards up, things settle down, and the boys begin to bowl with singular focus. Which frees me up to take in my surroundings. They've redone this alley since the last time I was here—faux wood lanes, big screens blasting entertainment, fresh carpeting, and a startling amount of neon.

Sawyer steps down the runway into a low lunge or stretch or whatever you call it when you release the ball—I know squat about bowling. He's so graceful in motion. He has dexterous fingers for someone with such big hands, and a surprisingly athletic and nimble body considering the amount of muscle he packs.

Mmmm.

The ball rolls true down the middle of the lane and hits the pins dead center.

Strike.

He turns toward me and winks, as if he knows I've been watching him lustfully.

"Your turn, Ms. Dunning," Griggs says.

I yank my mind back from where it's gone and send the ball down the lane with considerably less grace than my next-door neighbor, but the boys couldn't care less. They're too busy trying to beat each other to worry about the adults.

After a while, Sawyer and I drift out of our respective games and stand back, surveying our fiefdoms.

"You throw a good party, Paulson," I tell him.

His expression fills with regret.

"What's wrong?"

He shakes his head and ducks his chin. "Nothing."

I narrow my eyes at him—then get it, suddenly. "Lucy?"

Startled, his eyes come up to meet mine, dark with grief.

"You must miss her a lot, times like this. Birthdays, holidays."

His gaze shifts again, off beyond the neon horizon. "She

wouldn't have forgotten about driving the boys from the bowling alley back to the house."

I'm about to reassure him, to insist that anyone could have forgotten about that (or maybe I just mean I could have), when he bursts out, "Hell—she wouldn't have had a party at a bowling alley to begin with."

"She wouldn't have?"

Part of me hates that he's still so in love with Lucy, but the other part is aware that it's unusual for him to reveal his feelings like this, and I don't want him to stop.

He takes a deep breath, closes his eyes, then opens them again. "She would have done it at home. There would have been a theme, and decorations—one year it was a pirate party, and she turned the dining room table into a pirate ship with giant cardboard waves rising from the floor. She painted the waves with this blue glitter paint. She had the boys make homemade eye patches and homemade swords and scabbards, and then she let them climb up on the table and have sword fights. The boys loved it. That was how she was. She didn't do anything halfway—" He stops. "I'm sorry."

"Don't be."

My insides are all twisted up in sympathy and over-identification—I can't help thinking of Jonah, who had, and lost, Lucy, and imagining what it would be like for Madden if something happened to me. My heart lurches horribly at the thought.

Plus, on top of all the other emotions, there's this ugly knot of envy, because—well, because despite everything, I like this guy an awful lot, and he's madly in love with a dead woman who might also turn out to be Martha Stewart.

Cardboard waves? Glitter paint?

I'm. Just. Not. Crafty.

Madden comes running up. "Mom, Caden and Alexander are in the arcade—are they supposed to be in there?"

"Not really." Sawyer sighs. "I'm sorry." He rubs his forehead. "I didn't mean to go off like that."

"She sounds amazing." She does, and what else is there really to say?

"She was."

We stand there a moment. His eyes are still sad and abstracted, like he's looking far into the past. He tugs one earlobe, frowns, then seems to come back to the present. "I'd better collect Caden and Alexander." He shoots me one more look—one I can't read—and jogs off to retrieve his wayward charges from the arcade.

I stand, watching him, dazed.

I don't think Trevor ever would have talked about me that way. Like the most ordinary things I did were infused with magic.

I drag in a shallow breath, then another. I'm shaking, I realize. But it's not because of how much I wish Trevor had felt that way about me.

It's because of how much I wish Sawyer did.

Elle Dunning, what are you doing????

28

SAWYER

Elle and I drive the boys back to the house—three in the back of my truck, seven in her van.

On the drive, I barely hear the boys' rowdy Pokémon conversation in the backseat. I'm too busy chastising myself for going off on that Lucy tangent. I mean, everything I said was true, but Elle didn't need to hear it. After all, she went out of her way to help me on a Saturday— when she didn't need to. And it's bad form to talk about exes —even the dead kind—with someone you're messing around with, even when you're not technically in a relationship.

But I have to admit, too, that it was a relief to be able to talk about Lucy.

All those words, I think they've been waiting for a chance to come out, and Elle makes it easy. She listens without judgment. She doesn't push or pry or prod. She's just . . . open.

The other night when I came in her mouth, it felt like I was pouring myself into her. And that's what it feels like when I talk to her, too, like letting all the pent-up stuff just flow out, and she takes it in and accepts it.

But I have a bad, hangover-ish feeling about it now. Like I mixed beer and whiskey in the wrong order.

I pull the truck into my driveway and Elle is right behind me, pulling up to the curb in front of my house. Boys spill out of both cars, and we head up the front path as a pack. The front door opens to greet us.

"Uncle Brooks!" Jonah cries in delight.

Whoops, I forgot about Brooks. I'd mentioned the party to him in passing, and he'd muttered something about his work schedule and how much he hated spending time with packs of children and old people, so I figured there was no way he'd show up.

His eyes take in the scene, including Elle, and he smirks in my direction. Then raises an eyebrow, as in, *I need an update, clearly.*

I shrug. As in, *She's my next-door neighbor. I have phone sex with her and use her for her minivan.*

I suddenly don't want to explain the current state of things with Elle to Brooks.

"Well, look who's here!" booms a familiar voice—my dad. He's big, like me, six-plus and two hundred pounds, only with a crown of silver hair instead of my near-black. Until about five years ago, he was a really successful general contractor, but now he's retired and drives my mother crazy doing projects around the house that probably don't need to be done. "So who do we have here?"

Behind him presses my mother, no slouch size-wise at five foot eight, with long gray hair in a single braid, and behind her are Lucy's parents. They're the same age as my parents but look ten years older, and they're quieter than they used to be, almost as if they take up less room in the world. Seeing them squeezes something painful in my chest. They're the only people besides me and Jonah who know how hard the last two years have been, so when I'm with them, it's a blessing—because I feel understood—and a curse—because their grief multiplies mine and makes it heavier.

The grandparents greet Jonah like he's a celebrity and demand to be introduced to all of his friends. It takes a while to get the boys to settle down enough to make introductions. When the fray subsides, I introduce Elle.

"This is Jonah's friend Madden's mom. Elle Dunning. She was kind enough to help out with the logistics today by lending her minivan. I promised I'd reward her with pizza," I joke.

Lucy's mother's eyes are sharp. They absorb every detail of Elle's face, and then shift to mine with a question. I shake my head, a barely perceptible *no*—

Except I feel like a liar. I don't know about the rest of the world, but there's a compass in the center of my chest, and when I do something that veers me off course, I feel it, like a judgment. A nudge. The disappointed look your mom gave you when she caught you with your hand in the cookie jar.

There isn't anything going on between Elle and me, not anything that would give Lucy's mom pause, and yet—

I look up to find Elle's eyes on me, and I swear that before she turns away, I see hurt.

There's a stack of pizza boxes waiting for us on the kitchen island, and a big pink box that contains a birthday cake set off to the side, all courtesy of my parents. The boys dig in, hoovering the pizza at an alarming rate. The adults hang back a bit, jumping in only when it's clear there's plenty of pie left for everyone.

Lucy's mom, Diane, eats only one slice, then comes up beside me, at my elbow. She touches my arm. Her hair, which held only streaks of white before Lucy's death, is almost all white now, but her eyes are Lucy-blue. She's a beautiful older woman, elegant-featured and dignified. I curse the disease that decided that Lucy wouldn't get a chance to grow old. She would have done it so well.

"I couldn't find the birthday candles," Diane says. "Patrick and I ran out and got some."

"Oh, *shit*," I say, smacking myself in the forehead. Lucy wouldn't have forgotten the candles, either. "Thank you."

We arrange the candles on the cake and set it in front of Jonah on the dining room table. His friends gather around, and we sing to him. In the flickering light of ten candles (one to grow on), his face glows, and he beams up at us. "I gotta think of a really, really good wish," he says.

"It doesn't have to be *that* good," Griggs protests, impatient for cake.

"Let him think," Madden chides.

My eyes find Elle's, thanking her for having such a great kid. She smiles back at me, and warmth spreads in my chest.

Jonah blows out the candles in a single burst of breath, and his smile gets even bigger when everyone claps for him.

I cut the cake into slices and my mom adds a scoop of ice cream to each plate. The kids eat at the table, the adults hanging back along the walls. Elle's on one side of me, Diane on the other.

"He looks so happy," Diane says.

I know she doesn't mean to, but she sounds grudging, like she isn't ready for Jonah to be happy on his birthday without Lucy.

I'm ready for it, though. He's suffered way too much.

"He reminds me so much of Lucy." Diane leans across me and addresses Elle. "Lucy loved birthdays. She glowed like that. She didn't give a fig that each birthday meant she was getting older—she just loved that there was a day that was hers. On her birthdays, she'd treat herself to a massage, take herself out to lunch, buy herself a gift. And Jonah and Sawyer always took her out to Din Tai Fung, her favorite dim sum restaurant, for dinner."

My mom has drifted near, overhearing Diane. She puts a hand on Diane's arm. "We went on one of those Din Tai Fung outings. Lucy was like a little kid, she was so excited about the menu and about everything that came to the table." My mom draws Diane into a hug. "She was a marvelous woman, Diane. You did good. We all miss her."

I can't help myself; I look at Elle. Her face is—expressionless. Not angry, not sad, just blank.

"Help me see if any of the boys wants more cake or ice cream?" I ask her.

Elle casts me a grateful glance and we make the rounds, loading the boys up with enough sugar to power a small city.

"I'm sorry about that," I say.

She shakes her head. "Everyone loved her. They need to be able to talk about her."

"They think you're just my friend," I say. "They don't realize—"

"I *am* just your friend," she says sharply.

I want to correct her, but I don't know how. She's right, and she's wrong, and I don't want to make this too complicated or put either of us in a situation we can't handle. So I just say, "It doesn't feel fair to you. You're the one who's here.

You're the one who's helping out. You're the one who gave up your Saturday to make things easier for me."

It feels like there's more to say. About how she's the one who's been there for me and Jonah a hundred times in a hundred ways over the last few weeks—and not just in the scratching-my-itches sense, although God knows I appreciate that. She's made things easy that should have been difficult. She's made me smile and listened to words I didn't know were waiting to come out. Surely that all means something. Surely instead of talking about a woman who isn't here, my parents and Lucy's parents could be asking Elle what she does for a living, who she is, what she means to Jonah —and me?

They could have, if I'd introduced her as my friend, as someone who matters, instead of as "Jonah's friend Madden's mom who helped out with her minivan."

I want to go back and do the whole party over again, just to get that part right.

But what, exactly, would I have said?

"Would you mind," Elle asks quietly, "if I took off for a bit, just to get some work done? I'm a little behind where I meant to be this week . . . and Madden's having such a good time, and I know you want to be with your family—and Lucy's— and Jonah—"

She bites her lip, but this time, instead of seeing sex in the gesture, I see the vulnerability. And something slips a little in my chest, some resolve, some certainty. I want to put my teeth where hers are, yes, but what I want to do most is to take her in my arms and smooth a finger gently over the lip she's hurting.

"Sawyer."

It's Diane behind me. "Come help me stack the presents up for Jonah to open."

"You start. I'll be right there."

Diane tips her head to one side, eyeing Elle and me, then drifts back to where the presents are strewn across the kitchen counter.

When I look back at Elle, her eyes have followed Diane into the kitchen.

"You don't have to go."

Her gaze snaps back to mine.

"Stay for the presents."

She smiles, faintly, but shakes her head. "Send Madden back when you're done with him."

Then she scoops up her purse, does a quick round of polite goodbyes, and is gone.

"You're fucking her," Brooks says mildly.

The party's over; the guests have gone home. Lucy's parents have left, and my parents are tucking Jonah in upstairs while Brooks and I clean up the kitchen.

"What are you talking about?"

"Your neighbor. Ellie."

"Elle."

"You're fucking her." He gestures with the frosting-covered fork he's holding.

"I'm not fucking her."

Okay, that's a technicality. I *did* fuck her. And if all goes according to plan, I *will* fuck her. But presently Elle and I are post-fucking and pre-fucking, and thus *not fucking.*

"You want to fuck her," Brooks says. "You're going to fuck her."

The man can read minds. It is his best and his worst trait.

He crosses his arms and glowers at me. "Don't do it. She isn't that kind of woman. You can tell just by looking at her. The kind of woman you can fuck and walk away from is like dark chocolate. You know that cracking noise dark chocolate makes when you bite it or break it? That's called *snap*. Dark chocolate has snap. It has a strong backbone. It knows what it is. Ellie—"

"Elle," I correct involuntarily, and he gives me another look: *Oh, Jesus, man, you are a mess.*

"—*Elle* has a soft-and-chewy center. She's a caramel." He jams the fork into the dishwasher, following it up with another handful of silverware.

"You're a lunatic."

He raises his eyebrows. "Tell me you don't know what I mean."

I close my eyes, briefly.

"Sawyer, she's your neighbor. Bad idea. Don't do it."

"I think it might be too late."

Brooks stares at me.

I tell him about the wedding and the agreement Elle and I made. I give him a quick rundown of the foreplay situation, details omitted, just enough so he grasps the lay of the land. No pun intended.

"We both totally know what we're getting ourselves into," I say in conclusion.

"No one ever knows what they're getting themselves into," Brooks says. "Sex is like a giant black hole. You think you're in charge, but there's all this gravitational pull and antimatter, and before you know it you've been sucked into something that even the world's best scientists don't know shit about."

I eye him. "Does this have anything to do with that woman you told me you slept with and shouldn't have? Chase's girlfriend Liv's friend? Eve?"

"We're talking about you, not me," Brooks says.

"*Sure* we are."

"Don't try to change the subject."

I grab a handful of paper plates and shove them en masse into the kitchen garbage. He's wrong. He's wrong about Elle, and I need him to know it.

"She's strong," I say. "Her asshole ex-husband cheated on her in the worst way, and she didn't fall apart. She's raising her kid on her own. She stands up for herself and her people. Give her some credit, okay? She's not a caramel. She knows her own mind, and she knows where she and I stand, so mind your own black hole of sex nothingness and let me mind mine."

The look Brooks gives me now is in a whole other category. Like I just told him I've taken up ballet dancing.

"You *like* her."

I shrug. "'Course I like her."

"No, I mean, you *like her* like her."

"What are we, in seventh grade?"

"I just wasn't expecting that. I didn't see you getting over Luce anytime in this cent—"

"I'm not over Luce." My voice is hard.

Brooks puts both his hands up and takes a step back. "Yikes, man. Sorry."

"I'll never be over Luce."

My heart is pounding with anger and a deep, gut-clenching sadness.

"I didn't mean it that way." Brooks takes a step toward me and puts his hand on my arm. "I shouldn't have said that. Look, I think it's a good thing. A real good thing. It's okay to be happy, you know? Luce would want you to be happy. You know that."

I shake my head.

What I know is that it's complicated to give up the person you love most in the world, and knowing you have no choice in the matter doesn't make it any easier.

When Lucy knew she was dying—I mean, when she really, really knew there was nothing left to do—she told me, *I know you'll have to move on.*

We were home—in the old house—downstairs in the living room, where hospice had set up a hospital bed for her. Her hand worked convulsively at the thin sheet. *I want you to move on, in the good, big part of my heart. But there's this mean, selfish part of me that wants to throw things when I think about you falling in love with someone else.*

By that point, she'd been too weak to actually follow through on the threat to throw things, and yet, she grabbed my hand so hard it hurt and drew me in. Her lips were perennially chapped, her eyes huge in her thin face, her skin smelled strange and feverish, but I still wanted to be as close to her as I could get. *I'm pretty sure that when I die, the mean, selfish part will die and the good, big part will be the only part left. And all I'll know, and all I'll care about, is that you're happy. So I guess what I'm saying is, even if it hurts to think about it right now, I want you to fall in love again.*

She took a deep breath. It rattled, just a little, in her chest, like her rib bones were leaves blowing in an early winter wind.

Just make sure she deserves it. Because your love, Sawyer Paulson, is the best thing I know, and you shouldn't go around squandering it on anyone. Make sure she loves you like you deserve.

I pull myself together, swab at my eye with the back of my sleeve. I think I got something in it.

I glare at my brother.

"I'm not over Luce."

I'm expecting Brooks to back down, if only to avoid the potential of my losing my shit again, but he levels a stare at me that's surprisingly fierce.

"I get it," he says. "You know I loved her like a sister. There's no one like Luce. But don't forget I've known you your whole life. You've fucked a lot of women but you've only really liked one, ever, and that was Luce. So I take it kind of seriously that you like this one—Elle—"

He's gotten her name right, and he nods at me to acknowledge it.

"—enough to invite her to your kid's birthday party. To stand up for her when your brother calls her a caramel. You like her," he repeats. "You *like her* like her. And that's gotta mean something. So I guess I'm just saying, as your brother . . ."

He takes a deep breath.

"Try not to fuck this up too bad."

30

ELLE

After I get Madden to bed, I change into my rubber-duck pajamas, brush my hair and twist it into a bun, wash my face, brush my teeth, and throw myself down on the couch in the living room with a package of Oreos. My plan is to eat too many of them and feel sorry for myself.

I'm halfway through one row of cookies when the doorbell rings.

I almost don't answer it. I'm pretty sure it's Sawyer, and I can't. I just can't.

I can't stop myself from liking him more and more. And it was pretty clear to me today at the party that I can't stop myself from being jealous of his dead wife. And it felt so much like the way it used to feel to be with Trevor and hear him talk about Helen. Helen this. Helen that.

But I'm with you, Trevor used to say, when I called him on it. *Don't be ridiculous,* he sometimes said, when I told him I was jealous of her.

Only he wasn't with me. And I wasn't being ridiculous.

Sawyer's knock sounds again. He knows I'm in here.

He's leaning casually on my railing when I open the door. His dark hair is rumpled. He's wearing a gray T-shirt that's a little too tight (in the best possible way) and a pair of cutoff sweats. I want to grab him, haul him inside, and run my hands over every square inch of his body.

Instead, I say, "Where's Jonah?"

"Asleep. Brooks and my parents are with him. Can I come in?"

"I don't think you should."

His eyes move over my face, probing. "Why not?"

"I don't think we should do—this—anymore."

He doesn't seem surprised, which shores up my conviction that I'm right.

"What if I told you I just want to talk to you? And that's not code for anything else, I swear."

I hesitate. I worry that if I let him in, I'll let him kiss me, and if he kisses me, I'll lose the resolve I forged this afternoon. If I let myself have feelings for Sawyer, I'm going to be in a world of hurt. I'm going to spend every minute I'm with him knowing that I can't measure up.

He holds up a hand. "Five minutes."

I hold the door open and let him walk past me. I follow him into the living room, where we sit on opposite ends of the couch with a broad stretch of upholstery between us. Even then, I don't feel safe, not with how much I want to slide my hands under his clothes, feel the heat of his skin.

Or with how he's looking at me.

"Brooks pointed something out to me today," he says.

I'm silent.

"He reminded me that I don't like very many women. Or

people, period, I guess. I don't open up easily. I don't warm up. I don't make friends everywhere I go." He rubs his palm over the evening scruff riming his jaw.

I'm not sure where he's going with this.

"He's right. I don't feel comfortable with most people. But I do feel comfortable with you. Like I can be my real self."

A warm vine twines itself around in my chest (not to mention several other parts of me), but my voice, when it emerges, is still wary. "I'm—glad."

"And there's the sex thing. I've had a lot of sex."

"Yeah. I gathered," I say darkly.

"But I haven't had sex *twice* with anyone other than Lucy."

"How is that possible?" I demand, forgetting caution completely in my shock.

"Just never wanted to. Before you."

Before you. I feel breathless, almost giddy, but I remind myself that all he's said so far is that he feels comfortable with me and rarely goes back for seconds—which I knew. Hardly a ringing endorsement of whatever is going on between us ...

He leans in, face earnest, eyes serious, and reaches for my hands. "But I want to. I want to have sex with you again. I want it a lot. And it's not just because you're hot or good in bed, because lots of those other one-time women were those things, too. It's because you're you, and I like you."

"Oh," I say, trying not to get bowled over by the marching band blaring happy songs straight through the middle of my chest. I want to make sure he's saying what I think he's saying before I let myself join the celebration.

"I guess what I'm saying, not very well, is that I think we

should try to make this work. You and me. A—" He squints. "Relationship."

Despite the seriousness of the situation, despite how cautious I'm still feeling, I burst out laughing. It's the way he says it, the way some people would say *eels.*

"You don't sound enthusiastic," I say, both eyebrows raised. At the same time, I'm wildly hopeful. Because before he said *relationship* like it was greasy or squirmy or furred with mold, he said *you and me.*

He leans in, his breath brushing my lips an instant before his mouth seals mine.

"Mmm," I whimper, and I can feel the curve of his smile, and mine answering.

He breaks the kiss. "I'm enthusiastic about you," he says. "I just find that word *relationship* hard to say. Like *moist* or *bulbous.*"

I cringe. "You just killed my sex drive. Dead. You can go home now."

His turn to raise an eyebrow. "Really?"

"No hope for resuscitation."

"Not even if I do this?" He brushes his lips along the line from my earlobe to the corner of my mouth, and I shiver with delight. "Or this?" He tickles around the shell of my ear with his breath, then laughs at my moan. "What about this?" He lets his fingertips trail down the side of my breast so they barely caress me through my shirt.

"Maybe," I say, but it comes out a gasp, and we both know I'm toast. For good measure, he lowers his mouth to mine and kisses me until I make whimpering sounds at the back of my throat and wrangle handfuls of his T-shirt.

He pulls back for a moment, his eyes serious. "So? What do you think?"

"I think you give good foreplay," I say.

"No. I mean about giving it a go."

I extricate myself from him, slowly untangling my fingers from the soft cotton of his shirt and climbing off from where I had straddled him somewhere in the middle of the kiss.

"What would it mean?" I ask cautiously.

"Dinner with me one night this week. Going to Trevor's wedding together as a real couple, not a fake one. Evening brain dumps—*honey, I'm home, here's what happened today.* Lots of sexting. If you want."

"I want," I say, a little more eagerly than I mean to let him see.

But he doesn't draw away in horror. He smiles at me, a smile so warm and so different from those early barely-there quirks of his mouth that I need to hold myself together at the seams.

Then he does something I'm not expecting at all. He pulls me close and hugs me.

He's big and warm and when he wraps me up, I feel completely at home and completely—

I was going to say safe, but the truth is, it's really more like:

Scared. Shitless. By. How. Much. I. Like. It.

31

SAWYER

As promised, I take Elle out to dinner on Wednesday night.

We leave Madden and Jonah with Brooks. Brooks grumbles a bit when he finds out I'm leaving him in charge of both boys, but I can tell he's secretly thrilled to participate in their Nerf gun fight. He gazes down at the Nerf machine gun that Jonah has lent him, looking like a boy at Christmas, and by the time I leave, he's chasing the boys around the house, bellowing nerfy death threats.

Elle had offered to walk Madden over, but I told her I wanted it to be a real date, by which I meant that I would ring her front doorbell and escort her to my truck.

The truth is, I want the chance to start over and do things right. We did everything backwards—crazy monkey sex first, foreplay after, getting to know each other third. But now I have a chance to make up for it. I can take her on a real first date, woo her, seduce her, treat her the way she deserves.

She opens the door wearing a blue dress made out of some soft-looking knitted fabric, with a deep scoop neck. Her skin is pale, pure porcelain where the sun hasn't touched it, lightly freckled above, and I want to bury my face—actually, pretty much my whole self—in those generous curves.

Apparently, no matter how much I want to give her the first date she deserves, I can't turn off my body's caveman response to hers.

"You look amazing," I tell her. I hold out the big bunch of black-eyed Susans in my hand. Her eyes get big and her lower lip trembles as she reaches out to take them.

"You brought me flowers."

I think, *Trevor Thomas is the world's biggest asshole.*

She runs inside to put the flowers in water, then comes back, beaming at me.

That fucking smile. I'd bring her another ten bunches to see her smile like that again and again.

She gives me a once-over. "You look pretty great yourself."

I'm wearing a pair of gray slacks and a button-down shirt. Nothing special, but I'll happily take the way her eyes rake over me.

She locks up the house and follows me to the truck, where I open the door for her, then stand back and not-so-surreptitiously watch her climb up.

She's wearing high-heeled sandals that tip her ass up and make her calves even more shapely than usual. The flirty skirt of the blue dress skims her thighs, milk pale and so soft I can barely keep myself from reaching out to stroke the skin on the inner surface.

"Are you looking up my skirt?" she inquires.

Honesty is the best policy, especially when you've been caught out. "Yes."

She casts a wink and a smile over her shoulder at me, then flips up the back of her skirt so quickly I catch only a quick glance of red lace against pale skin before she hops up into the truck.

Elle has changed since I met her at Maeve's. She was subdued that night, sad, with a streak of darkness and an air of defeat. Tonight she is all lightness and fun, and I want to take as much of it into me as I can. Or—my dick hardens in anticipation—submerge myself in her. Not that it will happen tonight. I'm determined to keep to our schedule: foreplay tonight, the real thing this weekend when we have time to enjoy each other. Brooks will stay tonight with Madden and Jonah as late as we want, but tomorrow morning, Elle and I need to wake up in our own beds.

That doesn't mean we can't have a good time. I want the word *foreplay* to take on a whole new meaning for her.

Once we've reached Il Capriccio, I help Elle out of the truck cab. She jumps down and slides her body the length of mine, setting me on fire. The impish look she gives me— *meant to do that*—doesn't hurt, either.

At least she's affected by the contact, too. As she rights herself, her nipples poke through the clingy material of her dress. I want to reach out and thumb one to even greater attention, but I remind myself of my mission here. Best first date ever.

Il Capriccio is in a turn-of-the-century farmhouse, rustic but elegant, with cream walls, dark trim, and dusky mood lighting. We're escorted to a table for two lit with real candles, and I pull Elle's chair out for her.

"Thank you," she murmurs, sitting.

I sit across from her. The golden glow flickers across her

cheekbones and settles in the yellow of her hair, creating high and low lights I wouldn't have guessed were there.

"Do you know how long it's been since anyone took me out for a candlelit dinner?" she asks.

"I rest my case. Trevor Thomas is the world's biggest asshole. Shit. I just said that out loud."

She giggles.

"And you're the most beautiful woman I've ever seen."

She goes quiet. We both sit there with that sentence, and all that it implies.

It's like getting stuck in a riptide, the ocean pushing me forward and sucking me down and back. There's grief and guilt and loss, and then there's the simple truth of Elle, sitting in front of me, so stunning in the dim light of dancing flame I can't take my eyes off her.

She ducks her chin, her eyes averted. "You don't have to say that."

What's the thing about a riptide? If you struggle against it, if you try to resist it directly, you tire and drown. The trick is to swim sideways.

The way back to life isn't a straight line.

I let the grief and the guilt finish washing over me, and then I reach out and take Elle's small, cool hand in mine.

"You know me pretty well by now," I say.

She nods. Her eyes are still and bright on my face, her expression wary. I want to wipe the wariness away.

"I don't talk much."

She nods again.

"And I sure as fuck don't say shit I don't mean."

32

ELLE

We're done with our main course and we've ordered dessert, a molten chocolate cake with vanilla ice cream and chocolate sauce. I'm somewhere near the bottom of my second glass of wine, and he's been asking me about my writing, and somehow, I find myself telling him about the super-secret divorce book. He listens with typical Sawyer attentiveness, idly running his thumb along the edge of his wine goblet. My eyes follow his fingers, my body softening and heating in response to the caress. You know you've got it bad when a guy can get to you by rimming his glass.

"Hattie thinks I should try to get it published, but I don't really think anyone would be interested."

He tilts his head. "Why not?"

"It's pretty hard to get something published. Really competitive. And there are, like, a million divorce self-help books, and there was the whole *Eat Pray Love* memoir/self-help thing, and now there are a million of those, too."

"So?" he asks.

"So, I mean, I'm nothing new."

"So why did Hattie say you should try to get it published?"

I shrug.

He narrows his eyes. "What did she say, Elle?"

He's pretty scary when he's stern. And hot.

"She said it made her laugh and that—I guess she thought it would make people feel less alone with the whole thing. Like I was kind of making fun of myself and the situation in a way that was really accessible."

He raises his eyebrows.

I lift a shoulder. "She's my best friend. She has to say nice stuff."

He leans back slightly in his seat and says, "You know, way back when I was first starting to make furniture, I said stuff like that all the time. 'Oh, yeah, he's just complimenting it because he's my dad; she's just complimenting it because she's my wife. There's so much furniture out there, there's so much repurposed wood furniture out there; what do I have to offer that's anything new?' Truth is, you can talk yourself out of anything. It's *not* talking yourself out of the stuff that matters that's the tough part. I think Hattie's right."

"Well," I say. "Maybe so."

I change the subject. I propose we do "favorites."

So we do—favorite color, favorite food, favorite movie, pet peeve, that kind of thing. And of course, the longer that goes on, the dirtier it gets.

"Favorite sex position," Sawyer murmurs.

The candlelight and the deep rumble of his voice are like warm water in my veins, and I luxuriate for a moment before

I choose my answer. "I don't know yet," I murmur back. "Planning to find out this weekend."

"In the past," he coaxes.

I give it some thought. "Maybe this makes me boring, but I like missionary."

"Not boring." His gaze pins mine in a way that makes me vividly imagine exactly what it will feel like to have him braced over me, his face inches from mine, as he moves inside me. It's hard to breathe, which brings another set of memories to the surface.

"What you did to me against the wall outside the bar? That was—" Blood suffuses my face at the memory. "That was probably the most turned on I've ever been."

He sucks in a breath and nails me with another dark look. "Vertical's good." His gaze gets far away, and he squints briefly. "I think, like I said the other night, I'd also really like you riding me. You've got the sexiest bounce I've ever seen —" His eyes drop to indicate exactly what part of me bounces to his specifications—"and I would really enjoy lying back and watching."

There's something about Sawyer. Most men, if they said something like that, I'd think it was crass. Sawyer means it. He's being honest, and it's hot. And he's watching me carefully for my reaction. Words, for him, are foreplay.

My breasts tighten in the spotlight of his regard, my nipples beading under the thin lace, front and center, and yes —his eyes darken, noticing.

His gaze lifts, meets mine, and I flush, hot all over.

He smirks, then leans back in his seat. He looks more relaxed than I've ever seen him.

Happy. He's happy.

I'm happy.

I'm trying not to think too much about what he said earlier. That I was the most beautiful woman he'd ever seen. That he wouldn't have said it if he hadn't meant it.

But beautiful is just that. Just a surface thing. It doesn't signify—

I grasp at the easiest way to get my mind back to the moment. "Favorite sexual fantasy."

"Hmm." His eyes are sleepy, like they were at that first night in the bar. Heavy-lidded. "Used to be fucking someone against a brick wall outside a bar . . ."

The pleasure he's been coaxing to life in me spreads, like a good alcohol buzz, to my lips and to the folds of my sex, warm and tingly.

"Was that the first time you'd done that?"

His eyebrows shoot up. "Yeah. What, you think I do that kind of stuff all the time?"

I don't know, Sawyer. There's so much I feel like I don't know, even after all the getting-to-know-you games. "You said you'd had a lot of sex."

He winces. "Well, yeah, but most of the time back at someone's apartment, or at my place if Jonah was with his grandparents. I never felt like it was so urgent it had to happen right that instant, like with you."

That sings through my veins like a strong drink. I guess until that moment I hadn't been sure whether that night was out of the ordinary for him.

The waitress sets the molten chocolate cake down and lays a spoon in front of each of us. A generous scoop of vanilla ice cream is already beginning to melt over the dark surface of the soft cake. My mouth waters.

"Be nice," the waitress teases as she backs away. "I've seen fistfights break out over the last bite of this stuff."

The cake really is that good. "Oh, *God,*" I say, licking soft, warm chocolate off my spoon, the contrast between hot cake and cold ice cream lighting up my tongue.

Sawyer watches me hungrily, and it's not the cake he's got designs on. "It's not going to be a fistfight that breaks out here. I'm going to spread you out on the table and lick this dessert off you. Or, better yet, I'm going to make you lick it off me."

I squirm, pressing my thighs together. He's making me so wet. "Gladly."

"What about you? Favorite sexual fantasy?"

"Besides having someone lick molten chocolate cake off me in public?" I tease in a whisper.

"Mmm-hmm." His hum is rough enough to rasp like sandpaper over my nipples and clit.

I tilt my head. "Sex in your truck."

"In my truck."

"Well, in *a* truck."

"Have you ever dated anyone else who owned a truck?"

"No, but the fantasy predates you."

"So I'm your fantasy guy come to life." He smirks.

"Yup."

We both reach for the last bite of chocolate cake, our spoons jangling. We joust for a moment, then he stands down.

"I'd rather watch you eat it, anyway," he says, and does, his eyes darkening as I caress the spoon with lips and tongue.

Under the table, his foot presses against mine. It's just shoe leather on shoe leather, but it might as well be bare skin on skin, that's how deep the sensation travels in my body.

"Where would the truck be parked while we had sex in it?" he asks.

"Someplace dark and quiet. But not a garage, not a drive-way. Someplace we could get caught."

His pupils are so big and dark his irises are just a thin ring around them. He shifts in his seat, and I feel a thrill of triumph, knowing he wants desperately to adjust himself and can't.

Instead, he raises his eyes to catch the waitress's, and I giggle at the urgency in his voice as he asks for the check. He gives me a stern look, but I can't help it; I giggle again.

33

SAWYER

W hat kind of guy could ignore that kind of information? I mean, *seriously.*

There's a lesser-known entrance to one of the wilderness areas in Revere Lake, one that backs up on the lake but isn't typically used for recreation. The parking lot there holds only a car or two, and when you're parked there, you're not visible from the road.

We won't get caught. It's a weeknight, the truck is black, and this entrance isn't used much. Which is a good thing. We have kids at home. Neither of us wants our kids to have to attend Revere Lake High School under the shameful banner of being the child of people caught doing the deed in a pickup truck at the edge of the Revere Lake Forest Area.

That said, we could get caught, and we both know it. The knowledge is like a hand cupped around my balls. And I can tell she's hyperaware of it, too, because when I brush her long hair back from her face, she whimpers at the touch of fingertips on blond strands, telling me how primed she is for me.

I kiss her cheek—as smooth as satin—the whorls of her

ear, the edge of her jaw, the long line of her throat, her collarbone, until my fingertips find the top edge of her dress, and oh my God her tits are so fucking soft . . .

"I could live here," I say reverently, my lips and nose against the curve of her breast, and she laughs, then jerks away suddenly.

"What was that?" she asks, and I can feel her heart pick up.

I'd seen it, too, the flash of lights from a car on the road.

"What, worried someone will see?" I tease. I cup her head, draw her close to me, kiss her. Just the touch of mouth to mouth, then a slow, tentative exploration, my tongue seeking and finding ways to give her pleasure. Her lips nip mine, her hands tug on my shirt and hair. She jerks my shirt out of my waistband so she can slide her hands under it while I kiss her deeper, longer, fiercer. I want to know every sound she makes. I want her to make sounds she's never made before.

The headlights pass, illuminating the interior of the truck just enough to show me the haze of desire in her eyes, then head off down the road.

"We could get caught," she whispers.

"Mmm-hmm. We could."

She shivers.

"You like that."

"Yeah."

Jesus. "C'mere," I say, and she climbs over the central console, straddling me. She reaches between us, unbuckles my belt, fumbles with my zipper. I push her hands out of the way. She lifts up and gives me access, and I free myself. My dick juts up between us, and she wriggles close, rubbing herself on me. I can feel how wet she is, soaking through the thin lace of her panties.

"Condom," she demands breathily.

"Foreplay," I remind her.

"I want you. Now. Tonight."

I almost lose it. I have to summon all of my willpower. It has been worn thin by weeks of teasing each other, but we've made it this far and have only a few more days to go. I want the chance to make love to her slowly, carefully, luxuriously, on a hotel bed, for as long and as many times as I want. I want to make sure she has no regrets and no reason to distrust things between us.

"I don't have a condom."

"I think I have one in my pur—"

I cut off her words with a deep kiss, reaching between us to tug her lacy panties to the side so I can ease my erection along the slick seam of her sex. My dick skates across her swollen clit.

"Ohhhhhhh."

"Like that?"

"I'd like it better if—"

I kiss her again, thrusting my tongue into her mouth, and she moans, shifting her hips against my hardness. She's so wet we can hear that juicy slide in the quiet cab.

"I can hear how wet you are. I can hear how much you want it."

Her head falls back and she grinds herself against me again. Her clit's so ripe I can feel it against me, distinct, and I'm suddenly right at the edge. It's her, the sound and scent and feel of her, her moans and her enthusiasm and how much fun I've had tonight with her, and for a second I'm convinced I'm going to go over before she does, but then she grabs my arms and cries out, humping me almost violently, wracking her body against mine, calling my name, squeezing my thighs between hers, and biting my shoulder hard enough to hurt.

I think it's the teeth that do me in, in the end. I have just enough presence of mind to drop my palm over the head of my dick so I don't coat us both in semen, even though some primitive part of me wants to—

"I want to come all over you," I say helplessly, as I manage not to stripe her.

"Another day," she says breathlessly, still jerking against me, all out of rhythm now, her face wide open with surprised pleasure.

"Is there anything that shocks you?" I demand, coming down off the blissful wringing high.

She shakes her head.

I lean across her to the glove box, find the wipes I keep there, clean myself up.

She watches, eyes soft. "Sawyer," she whispers.

"Mmm-hmm."

"I feel empty inside."

"Oh, Jesus, Elle."

"Put your fingers in."

What's a guy supposed to do? I oblige, of course. She's still coming, still pulsing. Her hand tangles with mine, her fingers on her clit.

"God, Elle, you make me crazy."

She makes herself come again while I work my fingers inside her, curling them against her g-spot, my other hand tucking into the edge of her dress and bra to tease her nipple.

When she's done thrashing, she sighs and leans her head against my shoulder.

A wave of tenderness sweeps through me, and I gather her as tight as I can to me. She rests her cheek against my chest and her arms come tight around me. Neither of us says anything, but I think we're both feeling it, the intensity of the connection and something else, a giddy hopefulness.

We stay there a few minutes, and then it takes a while to get us untangled and cleaned up. Her dress hasn't escaped entirely unscathed. Which makes me perversely happy.

"Does that count?" I ask her, once we're all tidy and tucked in and I've started the engine.

"As?"

"As sex in a truck?"

She laughs. "Yeah. Hey. You never told me what your favorite fantasy was now that you fucked someone against a wall."

I love the word *fucked* in her mouth. I love the unfolding boldness of her.

I back out of our parking space, then turn to her, leaning close.

"Getting a girl off twice in a row," I murmur against her cheek, and can feel her shake with laughter.

34

ELLE

I make Hattie and Capria come over and keep me company while I pack for the wedding. It's one of those complicated-to-prep-for trips where I have to remember things like safety pins and double-sided fabric tape, and I know that between them, they won't let me forget anything.

Plus, I need to talk to someone about what's happening with Sawyer.

"Okay, so let me get this straight," Hattie says. "The sex is amazing."

I carefully lay the dusty-pink dress into my garment-bag suitcase, smoothing out wrinkles and neatly folding the sides over so it fits without making weird creases.

"The not-sex," Capria corrects.

"The not-sex is amazing. Even better. He's a great dad. Your boys get along," Hattie says.

"Stop. Stop," I say. "You're getting way ahead of yourself."

"Am I?" Hattie asks. "Amazing not-sex. Actual parenting

skills. Family compatibility. Fantasy fulfillment. I don't understand what there possibly could be to freak out about."

Capria raises her eyebrows. "Don't you?"

"Dead wife," I say. "Perfect dead wife who can do no
wrong because she's *dead*."

"Better than divorced wife who can make your life a living
hell," Hattie says.

She's speaking from personal experience. Within a year
after her divorce, she met a guy she really liked, but his ex-
wife was such a loose cannon that Hattie ended up breaking
up with him. There was no way on earth she could co-parent
his kids in that situation, she said, and as much as she wanted
love to conquer all, she was too cynical to think it could.

"I don't think we're really talking about the dead wife,
though," Hattie says. "I think we're talking about Helen."

I face away from her to dig in my dresser drawers for
pantyhose and a slip, making it take longer than it really
needs to.

"Elle? Don't you think we're talking about Helen? And
actually, we're really not even talking about Helen. We're
talking about *Trevor*. We're talking about how he lied in his
marriage vows and cheated on you and made you feel like
that was the way the world worked. But that's not Sawyer,
right? Sawyer's not Trevor."

No, Sawyer isn't Trevor, but that doesn't stop the tremor in
the pit of my stomach whenever I think about the possibility
of a future with Sawyer. I keep flashing back on moments in
my life with Trevor, times when he brought Helen up out of
the blue, then insisted there was no significance to it. That
one painful Thanksgiving when I overheard his mother refer
to Helen as "the one who got away."

The coal mine of pain that had opened under my feet when I brought his computer to life and glimpsed the size of the betrayal—and the scope of my naiveté and foolish faith.

Hattie crosses to me, takes a chiffon-and-lace nightie out of my hand and holds it up for Capria to admire, then folds it carefully into the suitcase. "This, my friend, is what you need to keep your mind on. Not your asshole ex. The fact that there is a man packing his suitcase a mere several hundred feet from here who, when he sees you in this nightgown, is going to come in his pajama pants."

I roll my eyes at Hattie's crudeness.

"Eyes on the prize, Elle."

I cross my arms and glare at her.

"How can you, of all people, tell me it's going to be okay? When you know how bad it hurts and how much it sucks?"

"Because you can't live that way."

It's Capria who's said this, surprising both of us. Usually she lets Hattie do the talking, but she's got her arms crossed, too, and there's a stubborn expression on her face.

"Sure, shit happens, and sure you might get hurt, but what are you going to do? You met a guy who can rock your world by text, on the phone, in a truck—"

"With a fox, in a box," Hattie interjects.

Both of us roll our eyes this time.

"Hell, he could probably make you come with a voice-mail," Capria says.

I think about that for a minute too long, and Hattie says, "He could make a fortune if that's true."

We all consider that.

"Do you think if we suggested it to him we could get a cut of the profits?" Hattie asks.

Capria ignores her. "And you like him. He's a good guy, he's a good man, he's a good dad—"

"As far as I know," I clarify.

"As far as you know. And you only know what you know. And we're all wandering around in the dark, right? So Hattie's right. Whatever happens, you need to have the time of your life this weekend. You need to pull out all the stops and bust out all the clichés. Party like it's 1999, live like you're going to live forever and die tomorrow, whatever."

"And pack condoms," Hattie says. "And lube. And maybe a dildo."

"A dildo," I repeat, my mouth falling open.

"DP. Just saying."

"I don't own a dildo," I whisper.

"Oh, Jesus, child," Hattie says. "You aren't really divorced till you own a dildo."

35

ELLE

Sawyer and I drive down to Portland together. On the way, I tell him I sent a proposal for the divorce book to five agents. I dashed out the proposal in an all-night writing spree Thursday night, fueled by Oreos, milk, and—I'll admit it—Kahlua.

He gives me a high-five and tells me I'm fucking awesome. I'm pretty dubious about the whole operation, but if both he and Hattie think it's worth a shot, who am I to argue?

It is a strange experience to check into a hotel with a man other than Trevor, the first time I've ever done it. But satisfying, too. Life goes on, and in better ways than I could have imagined when I said goodbye to my old existence.

We swipe open the hotel room door. Sawyer steps in ahead of me. His eyes go from the beds to me and back again. There is dark intent in his gaze. I shiver all over, but there are makeup and hair and other such things to do, if I'm going to be at my best at my ex-husband's wedding.

"I feel ya, mister," I tell him, holding up a *talk to the hand* palm as he takes a step toward me. "But it's three thirty and we have to be at the church before five."

"Later, then," he says roughly, his hand skating over the zipper of his jeans, not quite touching the bulge there.

I almost lose my resolve, but I remind myself that we have all night tonight. And that it will be all the better for the waiting.

"Okay if I commandeer the bathroom?"

"All yours."

When I come out, I am transformed. My hair is piled up with curly tendrils framing my face, I've done my makeup pale and smoky, and I feel like a princess. Or a sorceress. Especially when I see the look on Sawyer's face.

"That *dress*," he says. His dark eyes sweep over me from head to toe, gratifyingly hot, and I'm glad Hattie wouldn't let me send him a selfie ahead of time. It was indeed worth it to see his in-person reaction. When his eyes reach the bottom of their exploration, they snap back to my face, almost alarmed. "Those *shoes*. Do you know what those shoes make me want to do? They make me want to take them off with my teeth."

"Don't make the pink lace panties wet," I caution, then halt him with a wagging, warning index finger when he steps closer, as if to lay hands on the pink perfection. "No touch. Later."

His eyes narrow, but he obeys.

Speaking of taking things off with my teeth, Sawyer is wearing a tux, and oh, my God, he makes it look good. The tux shirt is perfectly fitted across his broad, curved pecs, the jacket looks like it was cut to order for his wide shoulders, and the pants hug his slim waist and hips.

I might drool a little.

We are going to tear each other apart tonight.

Or as Sawyer puts it, a moment later, "This is the best fucking foreplay ever."

He offers his arm gallantly, and we leave the room side by side. We ride the elevator down—managing not to do anything to rumple either of us as it descends sixteen floors —cross the lobby, and climb into Sawyer's truck.

He turns to me before he starts the engine.

"How are you feeling about this? Because if you don't want to go, we can just bail."

"That's mighty tempting," I admit. "Part of me can't believe I'm about to watch my ex-husband, who *cheated* on me, get married to his new wife, who he *cheated on me with.*" A flutter of nerves chases through my stomach.

"And the other part?" Sawyer asks.

I smile at him. "The other part of me says, *hell no!* No way I'm bailing out on going to a party with a guy as hot as you."

When Sawyer smiles, when he *really* smiles, it's like the sun coming out. "Plus there's how hot you look in that dress. And those shoes," he says, with heartfelt appreciation.

"And the whole *after-party* business . . ."

He starts the engine and jams the gas to draw out an unnecessarily loud roar, making both of us laugh.

Ten minutes later, we're at the church, and it's showtime. The minister takes his place, the music begins, and the wedding party processes in. Trevor comes first, on his parents' arms.

I feel a sharp stab of betrayal. Not just at the sight of Trevor in tails, but because his parents once walked him to the front of a church to meet me, and even then, they already believed Helen was the right woman for him.

They should have warned me.

They should have said, *He's still in love with her. It's only a matter of time . . .*

Two by two, the bridesmaids and groomsmen come down the aisle. Trevor's brother, Trevor's best friend—both of whom were in our wedding, too. A man I loved like a brother, a man I considered one of my close friends. I know they're not the kind of men who "take sides," but let's face it, I lost them in the divorce. They were Trevor's to begin with, and now they're Trevor's and Helen's.

Someone should have warned me.

Someone should have said, *He's marrying you because you're pregnant, but he secretly wants to get back with her . . .*

The processional ends and the wedding march begins, and suddenly, there is Helen, on her father's arm.

Helen's beautiful, and I don't mean it in a bitter way. She's *beautiful.* She wears a long, white column dress, with a high-necked tank, that most women wouldn't be able to pull off. You have to be really tall and skinny for a dress like that, and Helen does it. What's more, the dress is completely unadorned—no beading, no ruffles, no lace. Just Helen's perfect body and the dress. Her hair is in an updo, and her makeup is flawless. She glows as she floats down the aisle toward Trevor, and he looks back at her with adoration on his face . . .

He never looked at me like that. Not once. Not even at our wedding. I mean, he smiled at me; of course he did. His eyes were warm. But this is different.

It makes me hurt all over, and for an instant I want to run out of the church, get as far away from here as possible.

I should have seen the signs. I should have, should have, should have, should have—

I should have known the truth, and maybe there was a part of me that did. A part that knew that Trevor couldn't love me because his heart had already been given to someone else, that tried to warn me, *You will always be second best, and he will break your heart, in the end.*

But just then, just when I think I can't stand it, Sawyer reaches out and squeezes my hand. And this complete calm washes over me. Yes, Helen is beautiful. Yes, Trevor loves her in a way he never loved me. Yes, my feelings are bruised and wounded and battered and frayed, but—

That's all just ego, isn't it?

I don't need Trevor to love me.

I'm doing just fine. Madden and I are killing it on our own, and good things are happening—in my career, in my friendships, and with the guy sitting beside me, who is ten times the man Trevor ever was.

I have a life I couldn't have had if Trevor had been less of an idiot.

I take a deep breath.

"You okay?" Sawyer murmurs.

"Yeah, actually," I whisper. "You?" I turn to glance at him. And the expression on his face is...

He looks pained.

I feel like a selfish bitch for not having once thought about the fact that this would be difficult for him, too.

I squeeze his hand back, hard. And try to send, through my fingers, some message that will help.

While I try not to think about what his unhappiness means for me.

36

I gotta give it to Trevor and Helen—it's one hell of a party. And there's no way Elle and I aren't going to take full advantage.

The food is amazing. We gorge ourselves on passed hors d'oeuvres and the charcuterie and cheese table. We help ourselves liberally to the open wine bar, swapping tastes to try as many different bottles as possible. Helen's dad, I learn, is a winemaker—he doesn't grow grapes, but he bottles them.

We're seated at a table with a bunch of Trevor's friends, most of whom Elle is friendly with. I'm proud of her; she holds her head high and makes small talk with them, acting —or maybe, for all I know, feeling—like she has nothing to be ashamed of. And she *doesn't*. She isn't the dick in this scenario.

The beef is filet mignon, tender and juicy, with a side of just about the best garlic mashed potatoes I've ever eaten and stalks of young, tender asparagus. Elle has the salmon, and it's cooked perfectly, with a lemon-honey spice rub, and served with mixed wild and brown rice and broccolini.

And it's all foreplay.

All of it. The way Elle licks the rim of her wineglass just before she offers it to me, the way she looks teasingly up at me through her eyelashes when she drinks from my glass. The roll of thinly sliced salami she slips into her mouth, her tongue peeking out to lick salt from her lips. The expression on her face when she tastes the brie. The shocking expanse of her skin where the dress bares her back, the curves of her calves, the swing of her skirt, the keyhole cutout that exposes creamy cleavage, the spark that jumps between us when she reaches up to dab a crumb from the corner of my mouth.

The wedding cake has been cut and served, and I've eaten as much as I could cram in (the cake, like everything else, is fantastic). The toasts are in progress, and everyone's attention has turned to the groom's brother. He begins to talk about when Trevor first met Helen.

I turn to look at Elle, and she's pale as a ghost.

Of course. The time period he's talking about, the time when Trevor met Helen—that's before he met, impregnated, and married Elle.

What a horror show.

No, just *no*. She can't listen to this. But if we get up and leave now, we'll be conspicuous. Everyone will see her leaving. They'll see her fleeing.

I have to distract her.

Which is when I remember a very specific promise I made her.

I want to mess with you under the tablecloth.

Admittedly, when I said it, I was mostly just trying to get under her skin. Make her squirm a little at the Moving Up ceremony.

But given the circumstances, it's not the worst idea ever.

Under the table, I slide my hand to her thigh and give it a squeeze.

Elle has the smoothest skin I have ever felt. It's like satin. And there's just a little give to the flesh underneath, a delicious softness, before I feel the tautness of muscle. Her skin at the edge of her dress is cool, but as I draw my hand higher, pushing her skirt aside, it gets warmer, until I can feel the heat where her thighs are close enough to touch.

She lets out a quick, nervous breath, but I don't look at her. Her hand nudges mine as if she's going to bat me away—but she doesn't.

A little higher and I can feel the edge of her panties, then damp lace, and then my fingertips move through silken wetness, and now it's my breath that's too loud for the still room. But no one turns to look at us—they're fixated on Trevor's brother and the story he's weaving—so I keep playing. With the softness of her folds through her panties, with her lube, which I slick over every part of her I can reach, until I find the hard knot of her clit.

She squeaks.

I smirk.

She wriggles against my fingers.

"Hold still," I murmur in her ear.

She's having a hard time obeying.

I whisper, "You have to hold completely still or I'm going to stop."

Obediently, she goes still. She stares straight ahead, only the slight slackness to her lower lip and the dazed expression in her eyes giving away that anything is going on below the surface. And meanwhile, my finger moves in the lightest, sweetest, most tantalizing circle around her clit, dipping lower to find more wetness and smooth it over her. Every time I dip I feel the impulse zipping through her pelvis to push down against my fingers, to impale herself on me, and, holy hell I'm hard.

Just when I'm wondering if it's actually possible to bring her off this way, with no pressure, no penetration, and no way for her to control the speed or intensity of what I'm doing, I feel a tremor rush through the tense muscles of her thigh. I can feel her fluttering against my fingers, as light as butterfly kisses. It's the sexiest thing I've ever experienced—followed closely behind by the hot pink flush that covers her whole face and the keyhole opening of her dress. But everyone else's attention is so fixed on the wedding party that no one but me notices.

She's all mine, and the wild burst of possessive feeling that goes through me practically bowls me over.

Just then glasses clink and the room explodes in applause.

Elle and I lift our glasses, clink, drink, and smile at each other.

"Want to dance?" Sawyer asks.

What I want is to climb Sawyer like a tree, which I'm pretty sure he knows. But I let him take my hand and lead me onto the dance floor. The music is the usual upbeat dance stuff interspersed with a parade of everyone's favorite slow songs—so generic that I wonder if Trevor and Helen chose the songs or just told the DJ to "play stuff people like." Right now, we are dancing to "Wonderful Tonight," which also played, equally forgettably, at my wedding to Trevor, as well as pretty much every other wedding I've been to.

Anyway, the song couldn't matter any less. What matters is the press of Sawyer's big, muscular body against mine, the heat pouring off him, and the way his arms come around me, warm and protective.

I feel safe.

I feel cherished.

When Trevor's brother, Ian, started his toast, I tensed up all over. In all the horrible visions I'd had of this wedding, it hadn't really occurred to me that I'd have to endure this particular ignominy: Ian telling the story of how Trevor and Helen had fallen in love and everyone had known from the very first moment that they were meant to be together.

It was a story that made me, made our whole marriage, an awkward parenthetical in the middle of Trevor's tale of true love.

I wanted to run out of the room. I wanted to stand up and protest the unfairness of this situation, of being invited to a wedding to participate in my own humiliation.

Instead, I held still, and waited for whatever was going to happen.

What happened was Sawyer.

I want to mess with you under the tablecloth.

The thing was, there were so many reasons Sawyer could have done what he'd done. He could have done it for bragging rights—*I got my girl off under the table at a wedding.* He could have done it for his own kicks, because it was pervy and exhibitionistic and would go in both of our permanent spank banks. He could have done it because he thought it would warm me up so I'd be more receptive to whatever he suggested later.

But I knew why he'd done it.

He'd done it to distract me.

He'd done it because he knew it was going to hurt to hear what Ian had to say, and he didn't want me to hear it.

And I didn't. I didn't hear a goddamn word of it. I just felt the slight, gorgeous burn of his finger circling me, the rising tension that drew and drew like a noose closing around me until it swallowed me up. I came so hard against the light touch of his fingers that I thought I might actually have a heart attack and die. I was red faced and drenched in sweat and boneless from pleasure and relief, and I had no idea what words had come out of Ian's mouth, nor did I care.

Sawyer took care of me. He protected me.

He pulls me closer on the dance floor so I can feel every perfect inch of his erection against my belly. "It's going to feel so good to finally be inside you," he murmurs, bending his head.

This is a humongous understatement. The whisper of his breath across my ear and the feel of his cock against my stomach are turning me on. My panties are goners. My thighs are damp. I will be lucky if there are not beads of lube rolling down the insides of my knees.

"Can we leave yet?" I ask.

He looks around. Everyone is dancing. The cake has been eaten. "We can," he says cautiously, "but I want to dance with you for a little longer."

"Why's that?" I ask suspiciously.

"Because I know that once we are alone in the hotel room, things are going to happen really, really fast. Way too fast. So fast that I am going to have to apologize afterward. So I want to savor this as much as humanly possible."

I can't argue with that. I just lay my head against his chest, wriggle evilly against his hard-on, and make up my mind to enjoy every minute of Sawyer's brilliant torment.

38

SAWYER

I think most guys, or at least most non-asshole guys, make it a point of pride to last more than a few minutes during sex.

For literally the first time in my life, I may fail at this goal.

The instant we climb up into my truck, we are all over each other. Elle's hands rip my tux shirt out of my pants and slide up over my stomach and chest, then down to find me tangled and painfully hard in my briefs. My hands slip under her skirt. Her panties are drenched.

"Jesus, Elle."

We're kissing, open-mouthed, desperate. Our tongues tangle, battle. There's a band of pressure on my dick from my clothes, and that, the slide of her tongue in my mouth, and the memory of her clit, swollen under my fingers, make my cock throb dangerously, so I push her away. "God knows I want to kiss you more," I tell her, "but it would be really embarrassing if I didn't make it back to the hotel room."

"*I* didn't make it back to the hotel," she says, with a shrug and a grin. "I think it would be pretty hot. I could make you come now and then you'd have plenty of staying power for round two."

It's so tempting, especially when she grabs me through my tux pants, the touch both relief and its own form of torture. And she's right—I would have more staying power if she got me off now, but I want it like this, both of us pushed to the edge of our patience, to the edge of sanity. This is how it was that first night at Maeve's, and it was too fast, but it was also just right, and I know that after I fill her once, I'll be ready to take her a second time, slow and sweet.

Reluctantly, I draw back, peeling her hands off me. Just as reluctantly, she tucks her hands into her lap. We drive back to the hotel, keeping to our own seats. When the truck stops, we don't turn toward each other but instead climb down from our respective sides of the truck. We hold hands chastely through the hotel lobby, up all those floors in the elevator. We make it all the way into our hotel room, close the door behind us, and then—

"I'm not going to fuck you against the wall again," I murmur into her mouth.

She's pressed up against the wooden door, my body covering hers.

"We're going to make it to the bed," I insist.

She wrestles her panties, trying to tug them down.

"Don't. Don't."

She unbuckles my belt. Unbuttons and unzips my pants. Pushes them down, then my briefs. She wraps her hand around my dick, which pulses hard in her fist, so hard I have to concentrate not to come.

"Lift me up," she demands.

I do, and she wriggles like a madwoman to try to get what

she wants, but I'm stronger, and I carry her to the bed, where I deposit her, sideways, and kneel. I ruck her skirt up and press my face into her pussy. She smells unbelievably good, rich and fresh and salty, and I'm licking her like a cat that's got into a dish of cream, busy, hungry. My dick, freed from constraints, is throbbing and straining, but I ignore it, ignore the weeping pre-cum I can feel all over the head, ignore the roaring demand in my balls. I lick and lick and suck and nip and slide two fingers into her, and she comes with a cry.

"If you don't fuck me now, Sawyer Paulson, I swear to *God*—"

I fumble in my pockets, extract a condom, fumble again (with a few choice curses because even the pressure of the condom on my dick is a problem at this level of arousal), and oblige her.

I press in slowly. I know my time is limited, and I want to spend it well.

"Ohhhhhhhhh," she says, as I spread her. Fill her.

"Yeah?"

"Oh, yeah."

"You want more?"

"Mmm-hmm."

"That good?"

"More."

I slide farther, then farther still, then all the way home. The hug of her body and the feel of being seated deep in her push me closer to that looming, tantalizing edge. "Like this?"

"Just like that."

"Again?"

"Again."

Still inside her, I wrap my arms around her, lift her, and

slide her back on the bed so I can climb over her and look into her eyes, as per our conversation the other night in the restaurant. For a moment, it's steadying. She looks back at me, and there's trust there, and joy, and my attention shifts from the furious demanding pressure where we're joined to the sensation in my chest, like fruit ripe to bursting.

And then she lifts her hips, just the tiniest bit, and closes her eyes and opens her mouth, and the look of total pleasure, utter abandon, on her face does me in. Completely.

I roar my release, thrusting into her deep, twisting against her as I bury myself fully, watching as it pushes her past the edge again, the flush pouring up over her skin.

39

ELLE

If it weren't for the condom, I don't think either of us would ever move again. But after a while I feel him pull away, and then he rolls off me and goes to dispose of the condom in the bathroom.

I can still see the expression on his face when he braced himself over me and looked deep into my eyes, when I saw his emotions laid bare while he moved in me.

For that moment I could feel his feelings and he could feel mine. And we were both turned inside out, desperate with the need to connect, terrified, elated, falling without handholds or footholds, without promises or certainty, without a net.

It took me over the edge as surely as he could do with his knowing fingers.

But now, of course, I'm wondering: Was that real, what I saw? Or a product of my own brain, addled with sex hormones?

He comes back and stands above me, looking down. There's an odd expression on his face.

"What?" I demand.

"That was—wow."

I smile. "It was pretty wow."

He climbs into bed, wraps his arms around me, and draws me close. I settle my head against his chest. He's big and warm, and he smells so good, and . . . "I'm so . . . sleepy . . ."

I yawn, and it's catching; Sawyer yawns too.

"So sleep." He shrugs under my cheek.

"But—we have this room and this night. We can't waste it."

He laughs, a lovely rumbling under my ear. "Sleeping with you in my arms is *not* a waste. I mean, think about it. We can get each other off pretty much anytime, but how many chances will we get to do this?" He wraps me tighter, inviting me with a hand to loop my leg over his, which I do. It's bliss, the feel of his strong body the length of mine, and I let the feeling wash over me.

But then for some reason I hear his words echo—*how many chances will we get to do this?*

"You mean, because of the boys? Because of having to end up in our own beds?"

"Yeah."

He's right, of course. He's absolutely, 100 percent right. We aren't going to spring this on the boys until we're absolutely certain, and in the meantime, there aren't going to be many times we have the luxury of spending a whole night in each other's arms.

But he hasn't said "for now." He hasn't said "until we tell the boys," or "until we're public," or—well, anything.

Instead, he made it sound like he still thinks of this as temporary. A relationship yes, but not—

Well, not a *forever* relationship. Not a marriage.

Oh, Elle, you crazy idiot. Back the hell off. Calm the hell down. Live in the moment. Enjoy what you've got.

"You okay?" He lifts his head. "I can feel you thinking a million miles a minute."

"I'm fine." Somehow, I manage to make the word sound normal, even bright. And in case he needs convincing, I add, "How could I be anything but fine after sex like that?"

He makes a rough, contented sound. "Sorry it was short."

"Short, but wow. Anyway, you warned me."

"And I can make it up to you." He shifts under me until I feel his cock against my inner thigh, warm and heavy and hardening. "Unless you're too sleepy?"

See, Elle? He wants you. And he told you he wants a relationship with you. That's all you need to know right now. The rest is just you borrowing trouble.

About 92 percent of me is convinced. Enough to answer (honestly), "No. Hell no."

We don't fall asleep until much, much later.

In the morning, Sawyer orders us room service and we eat breakfast in bed. When we're finished, he takes my plate out of my hands, sets it on the nightstand, and kisses me. We have sex again, this time with me on top, for his viewing pleasure. It turns out to be my viewing pleasure, too. I can't look away from his face—blown pupils, a flush high in his cheeks, slack lower lip. Toward the end, he closes his eyes and tilts his head back, his fingers digging hard into the flesh of my backside. When he comes, he rocks my clit against his pubic bone and takes me with him. We give our hotel neighbors more audio than we were intending.

Afterward we shower together, where we review the positive attributes of vertical sex (less vocally than the last round). When we're both clean and dry, sated and fed, we hit the road. We have lunch in Portland at Bunk Sandwiches on 6th Avenue (I practically fall face first in ecstasy into my meatball parm, and he tells me that watching me eat is really good foreplay), then visit the famous Powell's Books, where I buy a few novels I've been meaning to read and collect a few sexy romances—man-torsos and all—as a gift for Mrs. Wheeling. Sawyer buys a couple of thrillers. Then we head home.

In the car, we swap firsts. First dance, first date, first heart-break, first time leaving the country, blah blah blah.

We're almost home by the time I suggest *first kiss.*

"Age sixteen, in the movie theater, Amy Orella."

"I'm shocked, Sawyer. Sixteen? I would have pegged you as a child prodigy."

"Nope. Slow starter."

"Hasn't held you back any."

"No. It really hasn't. Your turn."

"Age twelve, truth or dare at Kelly Simon's house, in the closet with Devon Santiago."

"Was it good?"

"It was awful. I almost gave up kissing for life."

"Thank fuck you didn't. That would be a horrible waste of the sexiest mouth ever."

There he goes again with the superlative, and here I go with the self-doubt, but this time I rush to fill the potentially awkward moment, not wanting to make him have to assert, once again, that he means what I know is just a flip comment. "What about first time you had sex?"

"You probably won't believe it, but it wasn't until senior year of high school."

I snort. "You were saving yourself?"

"No, but I really was a late bloomer. I was short and kind of pudgy till the end of sophomore year, and then it took a while for girls to actually notice I was no longer short and pudgy—and then it took me a while to figure out that girls actually wanted me. Once I did, though—"

"You made up for lost time?"

"I may have, somewhat," he says, getting a faraway look in his eye as he pulls up to the curb in front of my house.

I brace myself to say goodbye, but before I can figure out what that should look like, Sawyer asks, "Would it be weird if I came in and met your parents?"

He didn't meet them before the wedding because I ran over to his house to save time and a round of introductions (since I already knew Lucy's parents, who were the ones watching Jonah).

"No! It would be cool."

He cuts the engine and follows me up to the house. Madden answers the door. "Oh, hey, Mom," he says, like I've been gone two minutes and not two days. Jonah is, of course, standing right behind him. "Hey, Dad," Jonah says with matching nonchalance, and the two of them fly past us out the front door. My parents are right behind them in the hallway, watching them with amusement and affection.

"You can tell those guys missed you a whole ton," my mother says, coming forward to embrace me. She's a small, bright-eyed woman with a cloud of curly salt-and-pepper hair, cinnamon scented and warm, as she has been my whole life. I hug my father, too, who smells like coffee and the pipe tobacco he sneaks in the garage while my mother pretends not to know. "Probably the fact that we plied them constantly with treats. Grandparents' prerogative."

"This is Jonah's dad, Sawyer," I tell my parents. "Also my wedding date. Sawyer, my parents, Elena and Matthew Dunning."

"Very nice to meet you, Sawyer," my dad says, extending his hand.

Sawyer shakes it. "The pleasure is mine."

"Nice to meet you," my mom echoes, smiling at Saywer.

He smiles back. "You too."

"We met your in-laws earlier today. After the boys had run back and forth a few hundred times, we invited Jonah to come out for ice cream with Madden, so we stopped by and introduced ourselves to his grandparents and asked if they wanted to come with. How funny is this? We were all in Barcelona during the push for Catalonian independence, and we were probably all in the same square during a certain protest, maybe just a few hundred feet apart! Small world. How was the wedding?" she demands of me, without pausing for breath. Then, without waiting for an answer, she tips her chin up at Sawyer and says, "I'm sorry! I talk too much and too fast, but I get excited and can't seem to stop."

Sawyer laughs. "Now I know where Elle gets it." He smiles fondly at me, which makes my heart skip a beat.

"The wedding was surprisingly fine," I say.

"I didn't think she should go," my mother informs all of us. "I think it was classless of Trevor to invite her, and she should have turned down the invitation."

"Tell us how you *really* feel," my father chides her gently, but my mother just shakes her head and addresses me.

"Your father feels the same way, even if he wouldn't say it out loud. Trevor was never good enough for you, Elle."

Thank God for parents and their blind devotion. I so appreciate her saying that, even though I know she's full of shit; they loved Trevor when we were together and felt as betrayed as I did when he ended up with Helen. Hindsight is 20–20 . . . but again, thank God for parents and their willingness to back you even when you're clearly the losing horse.

"No. He wasn't good enough for her." Sawyer's voice is definitive. "He didn't deserve her."

I go a little gooey over that, and my mom shoots him an appraising look.

The boys fly back up the front path. "Dad, can Madden sleep over tonight? Pleeeeeeeease?"

Sawyer looks at me. I shrug. I'm thinking, *If the boys are in the same house, Sawyer and I can be, too . . .*

He sees it on my face, and he raises an eyebrow and smirks. He shrugs, too. "Sure, bud." He turns to me. "I'm going to head home for a bit, decompress, all that. I'll text you and we can get some takeout for the boys and us, too, if you want?"

"Sounds good." I say it nonchalantly, but secretly I'm all, *he wants to keep doing this, he wants to keep doing this, we're going to keep doing this.*

"Very nice to meet you, Elena, Matthew," he tells my parents.

"Very nice to meet you, too, Sawyer," they say in unison.

When he's gone, my mother turns to me. There's an expression on her face I don't like.

"Elle."

She says it very gently. The last time she spoke to me that

way was the day Trevor left. It's the Concerned Mom voice. "His wife just died."

"Two years ago!"

"Lucy's parents seemed to feel that he was very much not over her. They said he's still a wreck."

"He's doing fine." My voice is brittle. Defensive.

My mother fidgets, wringing her fingers. "They said he adored her. Doted on her. That he was destroyed by her death. They said they worried more about him than each other or Lucy's sister, or even Jonah."

"Leave her alone, Elena," my father says. "She knows what she's doing." He rests a hand on my mother's shoulder.

I cast a grateful glance in my dad's direction. "I know what I'm doing, Mom. I won't get in over my head."

But I'm remembering the wrecked look on Sawyer's face as he thrust into me, the shocking sense of connection, and how much I wanted it to mean that he felt the same way I felt, and a voice inside me says, *You're already in over your head.*

40

SAWYER

After dinner, with dusk falling, the boys join a group of neighborhood kids in a tag game, and race around until they're completely spent. They don't even protest when we tell them it's bedtime, and their lids are already sagging by the time they slip into their sleeping bags. We kneel beside them for "tuck-ins."

I ruffle Jonah's dark hair—noting that he's overdue for a trim (Lucy wouldn't have let it go this long)—kiss his forehead and say good night. As I'm getting up to go, he tugs my sleeve. "Daddy," he says. "If you and Elle got married, would Madden and I be brothers?"

Across the expanse of nylon sleeping bag, I feel Elle freeze.

I'm frozen, too. I'm not sure how to answer. Is Jonah asking if marriage would, factually, create brothers of the two of them? Or is he asking, obliquely, if such a thing might come to pass?

Trust a nine-year-old to make you have to answer a question you haven't even let yourself ask.

I wish it had occurred to me before this to consult with Elle about how we'd deal with questions like this. I realize, kneeling there, that we've made one of those dumb adult mistakes. In our heads, if the boys weren't aware that we were romantically involved, they wouldn't develop any expectations. But they're not old enough to really understand romance anyway. They just see their friendship and our friendship developing in parallel—and that's enough to make them ask questions.

I need to nip those raised expectations in the bud, to make sure that the boys don't get hurt if things don't work out between Elle and me.

"Yes," I say carefully. "If two single parents get married, their kids become step-siblings."

"That's what you guys should do," Jonah says. "Madden would be a good brother."

"I have no doubt at all that Madden would be a good brother," I say. "But please don't get your hopes up that that is going to happen to you and Madden. Elle and I have both been married before, and neither of us is in a hurry to do it again."

I let myself peek at Elle, but she is bent over Madden, kissing his cheek, and when she lifts her head, if she has an opinion about the answer I've given, it doesn't show on her face.

I push myself to my feet. Elle gives Madden another quick kiss and rises behind me, following me out of the room and up the stairs. When we get into the kitchen, I close the door behind us and turn to her.

"Hoo boy," she says, not meeting my eyes. "Wasn't ready for that one.

I touch her arm. "What I said—I hope you know why I said that—we don't want them asking us every five minutes if we're going to get married."

"Oh, Jesus, Sawyer, of course, that was exactly the right thing to say to them," she says, flashing me a smile. "You were a superstar. I was totally blank, but you said exactly the right thing."

Her smile, though, is fading, and there's an expression on her face that reminds me of how she looked the first night I met her, at Maeve's. Unsure. Well, fuck yeah she's unsure. There are still a lot of unaddressed questions in the room.

"It has nothing to do with you," I tell her. "I mean, it's not anything about you that makes me feel like it would be a long time before I'd ever want to marry anyone again."

"No, I know." She nods. "It's Lucy. And I respect that. A hundred percent."

"And it's not like you want to jump into anything. After what happened with Trevor."

"No. No."

"And I respect that." I reach for her hands and hold them. "But I do care about you so much, Elle. This weekend was amazing. And not just because of the sex. I had such a good time with you."

A smile crosses her face then, and warmth fills her eyes. "Me too. Thank you for, you know, rescuing me during the toast."

"You didn't need any rescuing."

"Yeah, well, it felt good anyway."

She looks like she wants to say something else, but she doesn't. Instead she squeezes my hands and asks, "Do you want to play a quick game of Scrabble or something, until the boys fall asleep?" She gives me a sassy smile.

"Absolutely."

She beats me soundly, and then she checks on the boys.

"Out cold. Snoring. Beached like whales."

"Wanna come upstairs?"

"Yeah."

I grab the bag containing the two books I picked up at Powell's in Portland so I can toss them on top of the already precarious pile on my night table and follow her up the stairs. We lock the bedroom door behind us and turn to each other at the same time. She rises onto tiptoes and I lean down, and our mouths meet, and just like that, so fast, it's like the first time—okay, the first two first times—all over again, like we can't slow down, can't get enough. Like it's been a year instead of just a handful of hours. The hungry way she kisses, the noises she makes, and the press of her body against mine make me so hot. She plucks at my clothes, ineffectually trying to get them out of her way, then her own, struggling to get herself naked, and I help her strip us both. She leans her head against my chest and I play between her wet folds, my fingers toying and circling and caressing, slipping and sliding in her liquid heat. When she's panting and trying to fuck my hand, I pull her down on the bed with me. I draw her on top of me and start in on her breasts—I am positive that if I am patient I will be able to make her come just by teasing her nipples, and I've gotten her most of the way there when she jerks back and says, "Now, Sawyer, *now*," and lunges toward the night table to retrieve a condom.

She topples the whole pile of books onto the floor, but

neither of us can stop to pick them up. I grab for the condom, because all I can think about is getting it on and getting inside her.

Once I'm sheathed she climbs over me, and as soon as I penetrate her, she comes, crying out, a flush washing up her chest, like she'd been teetering on the edge and that extra pressure and stimulation was all she needed. Well, that and the fact that my mouth is full of her breast. I roll us over so I'm on top and begin fucking her as gently and slowly as I can —as slowly as I can stand to, really, because what I want to do is push and pound and thrust and—but it's good, it's *so* good, because this way I can watch the effects of each thrust, each inch, on her. The little sounds, the color changes, the closed eyes, the open, startled eyes, the bitten lip, her hands clutching the sheets. There's a wild confusion in my chest again—lust and something fiercer and needier and way more complicated. Our gazes lock, and there's no way I can look away. She's asking me something with her eyes, and I try to answer. *Yes. Yes, I'm here with you. I've got you.*

You're mine.

I'm not sure where the thought comes from, but almost as if she heard me she wraps her arms tight around me, pulling me closer, pressing her soft cheek against mine. "Sawyer," she whispers, her breath against my ear. My chest constricts, but it's not a bad feeling—it's a sweet, half-forgotten sensation that makes me feel like we're connected everywhere, not just where our bodies join. Like we're one person, not two. "Oh, God, Sawyer—" She tips her hips, changes the angle on me, her breath warm in my ear, and damn it, I can't hold back— we both come, clutching each other.

Dimly through the spasms of pleasure wracking me, I know I can't let go of her.

I'm holding on in the vain hope of somehow not getting lost in the tumult inside.

41

ELLE

He rolls away from me, taking the condom with him, and goes to discard it in the bathroom. For a moment I just luxuriate, stretching out in the warm sheets, feeling the reverberations in my body of our intimate connection, the bonelessness, the full, sated sensation.

Sex with Sawyer is amazing.

Everything with Sawyer is amazing.

Starting slowly, quietly, that little bubble of giddiness rises up in me. The one that, if I don't try to push it down and squash it, might, just might, tell me that I'm falling in love.

And I don't squash it.

I let myself trust it, and it fills up my whole chest and does a little ecstatic dance in my bones.

Maybe, *maybe,* I could let myself do this.

I make up my mind to tell Sawyer how I feel. To ask him how he feels, if there's room in his heart for something new. Something lasting.

Meanwhile, I start, slowly, to pull myself together—I'm

going to need to go home; I can't be here in the morning when the boys wake up—and once I've found all my clothes, I begin picking up the books I knocked off Sawyer's nightstand. Most of them are just paperback novels, but there's one lying open on the ground, a spiral notebook full of handwriting, and I Swear. To. God. I. Don't. Mean. To. But I can't help seeing the first line of the entry spread out on the page in front of me.

Dear Lucy, I love you. I will probably always love you.

My stomach lurches.

I know I shouldn't, but I start reading.

It's dated six months ago. Before I met him. So that's okay.

Except my racing pulse and the sick feeling in my gut tell me that it's not.

Because I know, now: I am in love with Sawyer. And I want him to be in love with me.

The journal is a letter to her, his dead wife. He tells her everything that happened that day. What he had for breakfast, funny things Jonah said, even a question Jonah asked him. He asks her to help him figure out how to answer. He asks her to help him figure out what to do about moving out of the house they shared. He tells her what makes him happy, what hurts him, how much he misses her.

I can't bear to lose any more pieces of the life we had together. I am going to be one of those men who never gets over his dead wife.

My heart is pounding, and I feel sick. And I know I shouldn't, but I can't help it: I start paging forward, slowly at first, then quicker and quicker until I reach the last entry, which, like every other one, begins:

Dear Lucy, I love you. I will probably always love you.

It's dated three days ago. Friday. The night before we went

to the wedding.

He still loves her. He will probably always love her.

I hear the toilet flush, water run, and I immediately drop the journal back on the floor with the other books and go to the mirror over the dresser to begin straightening my hair. I am shaking all over. I can't stop.

"You're going to blow my mind every time, aren't you?" he asks, coming out of the bathroom, grinning at me.

And then, pausing, stopping: "What? Elle, what? What's wrong?"

I should have known I wasn't going to be able to pretend that nothing had happened. He follows my gaze to the journal on the floor. Picks it up. Clutches it to his chest.

If there had been any doubt in my mind about the meaning of the journal, seeing that possessive gesture erases it.

I turn away.

"Elle."

"You don't have to explain. You don't have to apologize. You were honest with me the whole way. I just thought—"

That all the little signs that he was still in love with her didn't mean anything because maybe he was falling for me, too.

Sound familiar? Trevor and Helen much?

I bury my face in my hands.

"Elle."

I look up at him.

"It's just a thing I do," he says, gesturing with his chin at the journal. "I write to her—a therapist said it was a good idea, and it is. It helps. I tell her stuff—I guess you saw that."

"I'm sorry I read it. It was just there, and I—"

"No, I get it. It's not like you snuck into my bedroom and started going through my stuff."

"I'm just being a baby. When you love someone the way you loved Lucy, you don't just—two years isn't very long, is it?"

He's shaking his head. "No."

"I'm sorry, Sawyer. I'm so, so sorry you lost her." My face is wet, and I can't figure out why. "If I could bring her back for you, I swear to God, I would. I mean that. If I could make it so you and Jonah could have her back, I would."

The moisture on my face is tears. I'm crying.

He takes a step toward me, like he wants to comfort me, then stops.

I gulp air, trying to slow the flow of tears, unsuccessfully. "It's okay," I say to him. To myself. "I'm okay. It's just—I think it might be too soon. For both of us. You still love Lucy, and that's okay. That's good. And right. And healthy and normal. I'm the one who's fucked up. Trevor did a number on me, and —the thing is, Sawyer, I just don't think I can do it again."

"Do *what* again?" he asks, looking bewildered.

"Be with someone who wishes he were with someone else."

He's frozen. And because I know him as well as I do, I can tell: He's thinking about it. Because he's Sawyer, because he listens, because things like this matter to him, he's really thinking about it. Asking himself if it's true.

The room is so quiet I can hear the hum of the heat pump outside and the sound of Sawyer's breathing, rising and falling.

He takes a deep breath. Exhales it in a long sigh.

That's when I realize I'm holding my own breath. Waiting

for him to deny it, to say, *I don't wish I were with Lucy. I only want to be with you.*

Of course he can't say that. One of the loveliest things about Sawyer is how truthful he is. How incapable of deception, of himself or anyone else.

"I do care about you, Elle. So much." He says it earnestly. Fervently, even. His eyes tell me he means it.

Something inside crumbles, the scaffolding I've used to hold myself up these last few weeks, despite my doubts. And I just barely keep it from showing on my face. It hurts enough that I want to wrap my arms around myself to hold the pain in.

I nod. "I know."

I also know what I'm about to give up. The best sex of my life, one of the best friendships I've ever had, the illusion that maybe someday whatever's between us would grow into something more, that Sawyer and Jonah and Madden and I could be a family. It's a lot to walk away from, but I am determined to build on a sturdy foundation the next time around, and that foundation starts with me being honest with myself.

It's my turn to take the deep breath and sigh it out. "It's been so good, Sawyer. So good. I'm grateful. I really am. And I'll miss you."

He closes his eyes, and an expression I can't read crosses his face. Then he opens them again. "I'll miss you, too," he says, and I can hear how much he means it.

"I'm going to, um, head home. Text me if Madden needs me?"

He nods. "Sure."

I make it all the way back to my own bedroom before I cry again.

42

ELLE

Madden is sleeping at Jonah's and Sawyer's. And, well, I'm not.

It's Friday night, five days after the book slide and breakup. Since Sunday, Madden and Jonah have zigzagged back and forth between the two houses as usual. I've kept myself busy with writing. I haven't seen Sawyer.

It seems ridiculous that anyone can get under your skin that fast, that you can go in a matter of weeks from barely knowing someone at all to wanting to tell him every little thought that crosses your mind...

It feels the loneliest at night. That's when I miss him the most, when the urge to text him or, worse, to run over and ring his doorbell is so strong I almost can't resist it. But so far I have managed not to give in to weakness. Each time, I remind myself how strong and self-reliant I've been since Trevor left. I was fine without Trevor, and I'm fine without Sawyer.

The tough love seems to be working. Each time I've felt close to spiraling into self-pity, I've watched a few hundred episodes of old television shows, deliberately filling my head so it can't be swamped with memories of Sawyer—smiling, laughing, raising an eyebrow at the sight of me in my pajamas and apron, pinning me with a dark look that promises pleasure.

Tonight, though, I can't settle. I try to do some work, but I can't write. I start washing dishes, then flit to the laundry, which needs folding, then find myself back at the sink (the dishes still only partially done). I feel aimless and twitchy. I try the usual medicine of bad TV, but that, too, fails me. I change into exercise clothes and go for a run, but I come back just as jumpy, and the hot shower doesn't help, either.

It just makes me think of Sawyer.

Lavishing attention on my body, washing me, making love to me with an intensity I've never known before.

Building a fence, thinking of me, wanting to please me with it.

Watching me at Trevor's wedding, knowing the best man's speech would crack me open, protecting me.

So, so good to me, but still not mine.

A dead woman's.

I blot my tears with my towel and run a comb through my wet hair.

I've just finished blowing my hair dry when Hattie and Capria text to see if I want to go to a late show with them.

No thanks.

Getting it on with the neighbor?

The words kick me in the chest, and I have to catch my breath before I can respond.

The neighbor and I broke up Sunday.

Forty-five minutes later, Hattie and Cap show up with supplies.

"Madden here?" Hattie demands, when I open the door.

"Next door."

"Red wine," Hattie says, pushing efficiently past me into the kitchen, setting two bottles down on the table. "You should have told us you broke up with him. Why didn't you tell us?"

"I was doing okay."

She eyes me suspiciously.

"No, really, I'm *fine*."

I'm not sure why I lie. Maybe because I feel so foolish for having deceived myself, yet again, into believing a man was emotionally available when he wasn't. I couldn't keep myself out of trouble even though I already knew what trouble looked like.

Capria opens a paper grocery bag. "We weren't sure, so we brought options. Peanut butter"—she puts a jumbo jar of Skippy beside the wine—"dark chocolate, marshmallows, Ben and Jerry's, Oreos."

I grab for the Oreos.

"Ha!" Hattie says. Capria, grudgingly, reaches into her pocket, withdraws a twenty, and slaps it into Hattie's hand.

"I guessed you'd want the ice cream," Cap says sadly, reaching for the Ben and Jerry's.

Hattie moves briskly around my kitchen, gathering tools. Bowls, spoons, a carton of milk, glasses . . . I pour myself a glass of milk and begin dipping cookies one by one, like a chain smoker, barely pausing between them. Hattie scoops peanut butter out of the jar with a square of chocolate. Capria doesn't bother with a bowl, just spoons Ben and Jerry's straight out of the carton. I would give them both a hard time about eating *my* feelings, but I don't have the energy for teasing. Besides, it feels so good to have them here.

"I'm going to eat all the Oreos first," I tell them, "and then I'll drink wine until I pass out."

"Before you get too blotto," Hattie says, biting her lip, "um, I talked to Eve today."

"Yeah?" I say, like a dope walking into an ambush.

"I wasn't sure if I should mention this—"

My heart picks up, catching danger before my brain does.

"But I thought maybe it would be better for you to hear it from me. She told me she's renting the house next door to you to someone new. I guess Sawyer's renting something on the other side of town."

"Oh," I say. "He didn't tell me."

Hattie's eyes are soft.

I bite my lip. "Of course he didn't tell me. Why would he?"

I'm not aware I'm crying until Hattie and Cap move in, surrounding me with hugs and comfort and lots and lots of tissues.

"Oh, honey," Hattie says, giving me a huge lemon-scented hug.

"Group hug," Cap says, and contributes coconut scent and a boa-constrictor squeeze.

When I get a hold of myself, Hattie asks, "Do you want to talk about it?"

I tell them what happened, how the journal fell off the nightstand, how I didn't mean to read it but did, how I flipped forward to find that the most recent entry was just days earlier. *I love you. I will probably always love you.*

"And you can't even hate him," Capria says sympathetically. "Because he's actually kind of a decent guy. I mean, any guy that would love his wife that much, and write her all those nice letters."

"Shhh," Hattie says, but it's too late—I'm crying a fresh flood.

"He can't be such a good guy if he's breaking your heart like this," Hattie points out. "I mean, he let you think he was ready to move on when he wasn't. That's not such a good-guy thing to do."

"He *was* ready to move on. Just not to let go. And he shouldn't have to let her go. She's not his ex-girlfriend. She's his dead wife. He's allowed to hold on if he wants to hold on. It's just—"

"It's just that you don't want to share him with her," Hattie says gently.

Despite her kindness, her way of putting it rubs me the wrong way. "It's not a matter of sharing or not sharing, it's knowing that I'm his second choice."

"Of course you don't want that!" Capria cries. "She deserves better." She aims this at Hattie as if delivering the zinger in an argument. "He had every chance in the world to tell her he was madly in love with her, and he didn't." Cap turns to me, all righteous rage. "You deserve better than that."

Hattie has a funny expression on her face. I know she's thinking about the demise of her own marriage. In her case, it wasn't that her husband preferred someone else to her—it was that he preferred anyone and everyone else to her, a fact that she found out by contracting HPV.

"Hattie?"

"Fuck him," Hattie says, her gaze snapping back to us. "Maybe that should be our motto? Fuck him."

"Do you mean Sawyer? Or Rob?" That's Hattie's ex.

"Or Trevor," Cap suggests. "Because none of this would be happening if it weren't for Trevor."

"All of them. Fuck 'em."

"Can we drink to that?" Cap asks. She raises her glass. "Fuck 'em!"

We toast, drink, and resume our attack on the innocent snacks.

43

SAWYER

"But it's better with four players! Why can't Elle play, too?"

Jonah stomps his foot. Madden wears a sulky expression on his normally angelic face.

"Elle's busy," I lie. My stomach hurts, not just from the untruth, but from the grief and anger that have settled under my ribs.

It's five days since Elle walked out.

Sunday night, I watched, unable to speak, as she gathered her herself, swiped tears back, and left.

I wanted to stop her, but I knew she was right.

I'd been so shocked when I came out of the bathroom and realized she'd read the journal. I felt sick, and sicker still when I realized why she'd done it. Because she didn't trust me with her feelings, didn't trust me not to be an asshole like Trevor.

And the thing is?

I *was* an asshole like Trevor.

Hadn't I said it myself to Brooks? *I'm not over Lucy. I'll never be over her.*

Why had I thought it was okay to offer myself in a relationship to Elle when I could still say those words out loud to my brother? Elle deserved a lot more than a guy who was emotionally two-timing her. And for me to be the second guy in a row to do that to her?

That made me an even worse asshole than Trevor.

So I let her go. I let her walk out of my room, out of my house.

I let her walk out of my life.

The boys are still staring up at me with small-man disgust. Madden says, "You didn't even invite her."

Jonah says, "You guys are just having a stupid fight and now we can't play Catan all together."

Both these statements are so true it startles me, although I'm not sure whether they know that or are just bluffing. Kids, man—they are the dirtiest brawlers. I shake my head. "Guys," I say. "We can play a perfectly good three-player version of Catan."

"It's better with my mom there," Madden says.

He is so not going to feel that way in four years, but it's very cute right now. Or would be, if it didn't make me feel like I've been sucker punched. Most of this week has felt like a sucker punch. I'll just start to feel normal and then I'll remember the look on Elle's face as I came out of the bathroom.

I can feel my resolve wavering. What if I just texted her? Told her she'd misunderstood, asked her to come over so we could talk about it. Begged her to forgive me, for the boys' sakes. Just thinking about it, about being near her again, the conversation and sex that would follow, makes me feel marginally less miserable. But then what? I still wouldn't be able to promise her any of what she needs, what she deserves. I still wouldn't be over Lucy.

No, we did the right thing. A little pain now to avoid a world of hurt later.

That doesn't solve my three-player/four-player problem.

I have a stroke of genius. "What if I call Uncle Brooks?"

"Yeah!" they say in unison. I think they think of Uncle Brooks as an oversized kid friend. Which may not be so far from the truth.

Uncle Brooks, who maybe should also be called Saint Asshole, answers my call and hauls himself out to play Catan with us. He's never played before, and he gripes a lot about how stupid and fiddly the game is, but he beats us all anyway. Vintage Brooks.

I thought I had the toughest part of the evening behind me, but it turns out I was wrong, as I discover when I head downstairs to square away Madden and Jonah in their sleeping bags.

"Isn't my mom coming over to say good night?"

"Not tonight, bud."

But it's not the same without her, and all three of us know it. It feels . . . uneven. Like she should be there, on the other side of the sleeping bags, whispering to Madden, looking up to meet my eyes from time to time.

I miss her fiercely, and she's right next door.

I trudge upstairs, feeling the weight of the day. Brooks has sprawled on the couch in my living room with a beer he's lifted from my fridge. When I come in with a beer of my own, he raises his bottle in greeting.

"How's your neighbor? For that matter, *where*'s your neighbor?" And then, because he's my brother and my best friend, even if he is an asshole, and can clearly see the expression on my face, "Oh, *shit,* Sawyer, what the hell happened?"

"Nothing happened."

"Bullshit. You look like I hacked in and deleted your season pass to the NFL. Did she dump your ass?"

I hesitate while I try to figure out the answer to that—did she? Or did we reach a mutual decision that we're a bad idea? I'm honestly not sure.

"It wasn't going to work out."

Brooks squints at me, brow furrowed. "It wasn't *going* to work out? Or it *wasn't* working out? Because that's two different things. You going to tell me what the actual fuck happened?"

I bring him up to date. I tell him how after I talked to him, I realized how much I did like her. I tell him about how we talked about giving it a try, how we went to the wedding together and it was—*good.* Better than good. I tell him about the book landslide and the journal and coming out of the bathroom to find her looking like she'd been kicked in the gut.

And then I tell him about Trevor. And what he did to her.

"And I can't do that to her. What Trevor did."

Brooks is shaking his head. "Man, some guys."

"I know, right?"

"But you know it's a totally different situation. Still having feelings for your dead wife and cheating on your actual wife—those are two totally different things."

"Yeah, but to her, not so much."

"Well, isn't that more about her than about you?"

."I just—it's probably for the best, right? It was getting complicated. Someone was going to get hurt."

Brooks makes a short, harsh noise. "Don't say I didn't warn you."

"I know. Caramel, right?"

My words are light, but there's a tightness in my chest. I'm familiar with it. I met it for the first time when Lucy was sick, when it took up permanent residence. It had eased for a while, recently—but I think it was just the distraction of sex with Elle. Now it's back, maybe to stay.

"Hey," Brooks says. "You want to go drinking with Chase and Jack and me Friday night? I could use a single wingman. Those two are no fun anymore."

The thought of it—of getting drunk, flirting, picking someone up, hooking up—doesn't appeal, but Brooks is looking at me with the closest thing he's got to a hangdog expression, and I can't say no. "Sure."

"We'll get you laid. Drown your sorrows. All that."

I don't even bother arguing with him.

"Elle? Elle Dunning?"

"Speaking."

"This is Jacinda Walters at Book Smith Literary Agency."

All the blood goes out of my extremities and I have to sit down at the kitchen table. Jacinda Walters is one of the agents I sent my book to—and not just one of the agents, but the one whose description I loved the most, the one who I've most let myself fantasize might be *my* agent.

"I read your proposal for *Splitsville,* and I absolutely loved it. I thought we could talk a little bit about what you're looking for in an agent, and if it seems like we're a good match, we could talk about the possibility of me offering you representation."

I open and close my mouth several times, but nothing comes out.

"Elle?"

"I'm just—shocked. In the best possible way."

Jacinda laughs. "Most people are. I rarely call someone and have them say, 'I've been expecting your call.'"

That makes me laugh, and immediately, my nervousness and shock abate. "No, not at all. But I'm exceptionally glad to receive it."

"Well, and I'm equally happy to make it. *Splitsville* is terrific. Are you working on anything else at the moment?"

I manage to pull myself together to tell her about myself —that I've been a freelance journalist for years; that I would love to see *Splitsville* find a home with a traditional publisher and be brought out in hardcover and paperback; that I'm not working on any long projects at the moment but that I have, in the course of my journalism work, stumbled over plenty of things I think would make great books; and that Jacinda is, in fact, my first-choice agent. At the end of the conversation, Jacinda offers me representation. She wants me to write longer chapter-by-chapter summaries, but once that's done (and I've signed an agency contract with her), she'll be ready to send the proposal out on submission to publishers.

"And they'll *want* it?" I blurt, then instantly regret it. Jacinda's being incredibly nice, but she's still vetting me for things like professionalism and confidence—the traits that would make a writer successful in the world—right? I don't need to let her know about my self-doubts.

Jacinda laughs, a long, delighted chuckle. "Absolutely. Why, don't you think they should?"

"Well, *I* love it," I say. "But I wasn't sure—do you think there's room for another post-marital-disaster memoir after *Eat Pray Love*?"

She makes a derisive noise. "Oh, hon, there's plenty of room. I was one of those people who just didn't get the *Eat*

Pray Love thing. It left me cold, you know? I could see what she was getting at, and I know there are women who say that book saved their lives, and I don't begrudge it, but there are plenty of women ready for a book like yours. Charming, self-deprecating, funny . . ."

I blush, even though she can't see me. Charming! Self-deprecating! Funny!

"I almost didn't send it," I blurt out.

Apparently my filter is broken. Or maybe I just like Jacinda that much. The last time I opened my mouth and so much stuff fell out was the night I met Sawyer.

But far from hanging up, Jacinda makes a noise of assent. "Writers tell me that a lot. I think sometimes the scariest ones to send out are the best. Can I tell you something kind of personal?" She laughs, almost nervously, which calms my own nerves, oddly. "I feel like I've known you for years, not like I just met you over the phone twenty minutes ago. Maybe it's reading your chapters. You build trust with the reader exceptionally well."

"Of course!" I tell her, meaning it. "I feel like I've known you for a long time, too." Which is absolutely true. If—as Jacinda says—I build trust with the reader, Jacinda's got a gift for building trust with the writer.

She draws an audible breath. "I'm eight months off a brutal divorce, and it was *really* healing to read your chapters."

Oh. Of all the things I was expecting, somehow this was not it. I've *helped* someone. And it means something to me that Jacinda wants *Splitsville* not just because she thinks a publisher will want to buy it or she'll make money if readers flock to it, but because she has a personal connection to it. To me. The realization comes with a wash of warmth. "I'm, um, glad to hear it," I say. "I'm *really* glad to hear it."

"I think your book is going to help a lot of women. Maybe even on the same scale as *Eat Pray Love.*"

Holy. Shit.

"But you said you almost didn't send it," Jacinda says. "What changed your mind?"

"My friends. My BFF kept harassing me, and then—this guy I was dating—"

It doesn't seem to properly sum Sawyer up, in any way, shape, or form. We were never really *dating.* And he was never just "this guy." But whatever. I plunge onward. "I was telling him all the reasons I didn't think anyone would be interested in the book, and he convinced me not to let that stop me."

"Smart man," Jacinda says.

I flash back to that night: the two of us, together at Il Capriccio. I can feel the strength of his interest in what I'm telling him and the depth of his faith in me. I can see his strong, rugged features, his broad shoulders, and when he leans in to earnestly address me, I can even smell his cologne.

I can hear his voice, too, the low rumble of it.

I miss him. I hate that it's true, but I miss him so much.

"He said, 'You can talk yourself out of anything.' And I realized that's what I was doing."

"You were shooting yourself down before you could get rejected," Jacinda says knowingly. "Happens all the time. In fact, it's one of my jobs not to let authors do that."

Authors. If my book gets published, I'll be an *author,* not just a writer.

"Well," says Jacinda. "Whatever chain of events led to

your sending *Splitsville* to me, I'm grateful for it. You take your time thinking about my offer of representation. As much as I hate to give you this advice, you might want to check in with some of the other agents you sent it out to, because sometimes if they know someone's made an offer of representation, that will prompt them to, or at least to read it. But obviously I very much hope you'll choose me."

Of course, I'll do what she's suggested, but in my heart I know someone else would have to really blow me away for me to choose that person over Jacinda. I don't say that, though. I just say, "You've been really wonderful. I'll think it over, and I'll let you know as soon as I can."

And then I hang up and dance like a lunatic around the kitchen.

When I've calmed down, I review the conversation in my head. It was so much goodness at once, I'm completely overwhelmed. I dwell first on the things she said about *Splitsville* —that she loved it, that it had helped heal her, that it would help other women. That it was charming, self-deprecating, and funny.

Whatever chain of events led to your sending Splitsville *to me, I'm grateful for it.*

Hattie! I had to tell her.

And Sawyer. I wanted, desperately, to tell him. *You can talk yourself out of anything. It's not talking yourself out of the stuff that matters that's the tough part.* He was part of the chain of events that had led me to Jacinda . . .

What had Jacinda said?

You were shooting yourself down before you could get rejected.

I freeze, and my hands feel suddenly cold.

You can talk yourself out of anything.

You were shooting yourself down before you could get rejected.

I mentally travel back to that night, trying to see the scene through objective eyes. The journal on the floor, the journal in my hands. My words, and his. What had I said?

You don't have to explain. You don't have to apologize. You were honest with me the whole way. I just thought—

When you love someone the way you loved Lucy, you don't just—two years isn't very long, is it?

I think it might be too soon. For both of us. You still love Lucy, and that's okay.

The thing is, Sawyer, I just don't think I can do it again—be with someone who wishes he were with someone else.

And what had he said?

Almost nothing. He'd answered "no" to my question about two years. And he'd told me he cared about me—even after I told him I didn't think I could be with him.

He'd told me he'd miss me.

And that expression had flashed across his face, which I hadn't recognized at the time but which could have—easily—been hurt.

Oh. God.

Oh God oh God oh God oh God.

45

The doorbell rings and my heart leaps into my throat, falls out of my mouth, and bounces down the hall. No. Not really. It just feels like it.

The doorbell has rung only a handful of times since Elle and I broke up three weeks ago, and every single time I'm taken hostage by my physical response. Madden no longer rings, he just barges in, but a huge assortment of people, ranging from Mrs. Wheeling next door to the postal delivery officer to the Girl Scouts, have rung my doorbell and nearly killed me.

This time it's Brooks with an armful of cardboard boxes, and I can't help myself—I give him a dirty look.

"What?! I'm here to be useful. I brought boxes from the store. For your packing."

"I thought you might be someone else."

He raises his eyebrows. "You thought I was Elle."

I sigh, heavily.

Jonah patters down the stairs. "Hi, Uncle Brooks! What's those?"

I see disaster coming a moment too late, try desperately to signal to Brooks, and fail.

"Boxes. For packing," Brooks says cheerfully, unwittingly.

Jonah may be only nine years old, but he's no dummy. His gaze swings to me, his eyes already full of confusion and anger. "We're *moving*?"

I've been meaning to tell him. In fact, I was planning to take him and Madden out for ice cream this afternoon and break it to both of them together.

I suck in a deep breath and manage to wedge my words in ahead of his next burst of outrage. "We're not moving far, Jonah. Just across town. You'll still go to the same school. And Madden can come over anytime."

"But he can't walk over. We can't walk to each other's houses all the time. We won't take the bus to school together." A ragged edge is creeping into his anger; another couple of sentences and he'll be in tears.

I wince. "That's true, but—" I'm about to launch into my semi-prepared speech, about how I'll drive him to Madden's house whenever he wants, pick up Madden at his house, how they can take the bus home together. *It'll be just the same as it is now,* I was planning to tell him.

A lie. A convenient parental lie. But what else can I do?

He stomps his foot. Hard. "I'm *not moving.* I like it here. This is where we're supposed to live. Madden is here. And Elle. And if you would just stop having your dumb *fight* with her, everything would be fine. You're acting like a *kid.*" His face is red with anger. "No, that's insulting to kids. Kids are better at fixing problems than you are."

He storms out and runs hell-bent for leather toward Madden's house, disappearing inside without knocking.

Given how well he and Madden handled the situation at school, he may have a point.

Thinking about that, about the friendship that grew up between the two boys without any effort at all, wrenches me back to reality. Of course it won't be the same if we move across town. Who did I think I was fooling?

Jesus, what an asshole I've been, to put off telling him so long. Suddenly I'm furious with myself, and not just for that.

"Nice job, Dad," Brooks says.

I round on him. "Thanks. Thanks a fuck-ton. That's just what I need right now." I leave him standing on the stoop, still clutching his armful of boxes.

He follows me into the house, kicking the door shut behind him and dropping the boxes. "The boy has a point, Sawyer."

"Shut *up*." I put my hands on the kitchen counter, bracing myself. I'm going to fly apart, pieces of me sailing off into space.

"No, seriously, dude, what's the big rush? Why do you have to bail out of this house? I thought you loved this neighborhood. You've done all this work—" He gestures at the recently refinished living room floor, visible through the kitchen doorway, and the new kitchen countertops and cabinet doors, which I've been working round the clock to finish. "Jonah's obviously happy here. It's not like she's going to come over here and suck you back in." He snorts. "No matter how much you wish she would."

My chest feels like an overinflated tire; I'm too young for a heart attack, right? "Is there a reason you're still in my house?" I inquire, as politely as I can.

"Is that any way to treat a guy who just brought you cardboard boxes? And I'll help you pack up the kitchen, too, if you're nice to me."

"As long as you promise not to talk."

"No can do," Brooks says. He comes around the other side of the kitchen island so I have no choice but to stare at his ugly mug. "Seriously, Sawyer. What's this move about? You've got cheap rent, you live in a great neighborhood, you love the elementary school, Jonah loves Madden—are things so awkward with her you have to run across town? What are you running away from?"

"I'm not—I'm not running—"

But I can't choke the words out. My throat's so tight, suddenly, I can barely breathe. Brooks must realize something's wrong, because he comes around to my side, touches my arm. "Dude, you okay? Oh, Jesus, Sawyer—"

Brooks's voice is alarmed—panicky.

"C'mon, man, don't cry—you know I can't stand that shit. For me, man, don't."

"I'm not crying," I insist, damply.

"Just don't think I'm getting you tissues or anything."

"No. No tissues." I swipe the back of my arm across my eyes and pull myself together. "I just miss her, you know?"

"We all miss her," Brooks says quietly. "But falling in love with someone else, it's not going to make Lucy, um, *more dead,* you know what I'm saying?"

Strangely, I did. I really did. I nod.

"I mean, I know it must feel really weird to be moving on without her, but I know she'd want you to be happy, and I bet she'd like Elle. Or she'd like how much *you* like Elle, at least. Jesus, I suck at this shit. How did I pull this job? I was just supposed to be dropping off cardboard boxes." He throws his hands up, with the intended effect—I laugh, weakly.

"And Elle's not dead," Brooks continues.

I look at him, startled.

"She's next door. She's right fucking there, dude. No, no, no, that's not supposed to make you feel worse—oh, *shit,* Sawyer, I'm going to have to go get the tissues, aren't I?"

And Saint Asshole, to his very great credit, does just that. Or, you know, the man equivalent, which is to bring me a whole roll of TP from the nearest bathroom. I wipe my face and blow my nose.

"It's just all mixed up, if you know what I mean," I say, sounding very much like a nine-year-old, because, let's face it, when we fall apart, when the big shit hits the big fan, we are all nine-year-olds. "I don't *want* to love Elle."

"Because it hurts like a mofo," says Brooks sagely, as if I've just said red is red or two plus two is four. "Every time you look at her and feel how crazy you are about her—and it's obvious to anyone in their right mind you are—your snake brain just throws up a big ol' wall, because loving someone that much means they're going to die and wreck you, and— who can blame you for not wanting any of that? But unfuck-ingfortunately, this is one of those choices you don't get to make. You didn't get to make the choice about Lucy dying and you don't get to make a choice about loving Elle. You just *do.*"

This is so completely and totally true that I actually manage a real laugh, which loosens the awful tightness in my chest, just a little. I poach a little more TP from the shrinking roll and try to mop my eyes as discreetly as possible, but it's not like I'm fooling Brooks.

"I'm crazy about her, huh?" I ask.

"You know you are."

I do. I don't want to be crazy about her, like Brooks said, and like he said, I don't have a fucking choice in the matter. I only have a choice about what I do about it.

"So what you're saying is, I should get my ass over there and tell her that I love her and that I want to be with her."

He puts a finger to the end of his nose and points it at me.

And then, just in case I didn't get the message, he throws the zinger at me. "Because life is short, Sawyer. That's the whole point of your pain. To remind you that life is way too fucking short. And if you ignore the reminder, it's just fucking pain."

That's when the doorbell rings.

46

ELLE

The door swings slowly open.

Sawyer stands in the doorway, nearly filling it. I always forget how big he is. Every time, it's the best kind of surprise, one I feel first in my body.

Please tell me it's not too late. Please tell me I can explain, ask for clarification, lay everything on the table, unravel the mess I've made.

I'm not sure who, exactly, I'm pleading to, but I hope They're listening.

Sawyer eyes me cautiously, but he doesn't look like he's about to slam the door in my face.

"If it isn't the devil," a voice says dryly from behind him.

I wince. I'm sure I'm not Sawyer's brother's favorite person.

"Shut up, Brooks," Sawyer says. "You were just leaving, weren't you?"

Brooks raises an eyebrow. "I was. But now I might stick around and spectate . . ."

I can't say I don't deserve it, but I desperately want Brooks to get the hell out of here and give me a shot at explaining myself.

"I could come back another time," I offer, but Sawyer and Brooks, at exactly the same time, say, "No."

Brooks claps his brother on the back. "Don't do anything I wouldn't do."

I wonder if that's code for, *Stick to your guns, bro.*

Sawyer and I watch him walk down the path to his truck, then we turn back toward each other. He won't quite meet my eye, which—well, I can't exactly blame him.

"I—got you something." I don't have a brilliant plan, just an apology gift and a lot of hope.

"What's that?"

"Maybe you should come see?"

He looks suspicious, but I lead him out the door and around the side of my house, and he follows.

I stop in front of a pile of wood, carefully stacked on pallets next to my foundation, then turn to face him. I want to see his expression when he realizes what it is.

"Holy *crap*," he says. "What *is* that?"

"It's the bar—what's left of the old bar—at Maeve's. Do you remember they were renovating Maeve's the night we were there?"

His eyes meet mine, and I see a flash of memory in them. I feel it as heat. He remembers, all right.

Hope rises.

"It's all they had left. There were wall joists and floor-boards originally, and a bunch of other stuff, but I didn't get there in time. But they still had the lumber from the bar because someone said they wanted it and then never came to pick it up. So they let me take it."

His expression is alert.

"It's a gift for you. An apology gift. Because I was such an idiot the night I saw your Lucy journal. I just talked and talked and I never bothered to listen." My voice cracks, betraying all the emotion I'm holding back. "I hope you can forgive me, and at the very least we can still be friends."

His eyes search my face. "Friends," he says, evenly. "Is that what you want?" He doesn't wait for my answer. He kneels and examines the reclaimed wood. "Shit, Elle, some of this is bird's-eye maple."

"Is it?"

"And the oak's beautiful, too. Jesus, this is—"

He looks up at me, his eyes full of something I can't quite read. A big emotion. "This is too much. You don't have to buy my friendship."

"It's not that." I can hardly look at him, for fear he'll see the size of my hopes.

I didn't make a plan for what I was going to say. I figured I would open my mouth and a whole lot of stuff would fall out, and some of it would be the right stuff. Now that seems crazy, but here I am, so, well, I open my mouth.

"I got an agent. I sent my book to a bunch of agents, and one of them wants to represent me."

"That's so great, Elle." Still crouched beside the reclaimed wood, he raises a hand to high-five me.

"Jacinda Walters, at Book Smith. She's amazing. And you were right, Sawyer. About how you—I—can talk myself out of anything. I was talking myself out of *Splitsville*—that's what I'm calling my book—telling myself I wasn't good enough, the book wasn't good enough, without giving it, or me, a chance."

He doesn't say "I told you so." He just nods.

Sawyer listens better than anyone I know.

"I told Jacinda the story, of what you said about it, and she knew exactly what I meant, because I guess writers do it all the time. She said, 'You were shooting yourself down before you could get rejected.' And I realized—" I stop. It's hard to speak because my chest and throat are so tight. "I realized that's what I was doing with you. Telling myself you were going to reject me. Maybe you are still in love with Lucy, and there's no room in your life for me, and no matter what I do that won't change, and years from now I'll realize it was like with Trevor, where I was waiting and waiting to know that I was the one—"

"Elle," he says quietly. "Shut up."

I do, clamping my lips together.

He stands, reluctantly letting his hands slide away from where they're caressing the bird's-eye maple. His gaze catches and holds mine, earnest and intense and so, so Sawyer. "I will probably always love Lucy. I mean, I don't exactly know how this stuff works, but I lost my grandmother when I was fifteen and I still love *her*." He takes a deep breath. "But there is room in my life for you."

He lets me take that in—on a giant wave of relief and joy —before he says, "And not just room, but the big bedroom, if you know what I mean." One side of his mouth tips up, and then, like the rest can't resist following, he grins at me.

I do. I do. I know what he means with a big bubble of hope and excitement that expands in my chest as he talks.

He takes a step toward me, opens his arms, and I fly into them. He hugs me—just hugs me—and oh, my God, it feels so good. He is so big and so strong and so warm, and he just holds on and holds on, and, "Even if you never want to have any more sex with me, will you at least hug me from time to time?" I blurt.

He shakes with laughter against me. "You are shit out of luck if you think I'm going to never want to have sex with you."

Then he kisses me, soft and sweet and brief, before coming back for seconds with gusto—and tongue.

If we weren't in the backyard, if Jonah and Madden weren't playing in my basement and liable to appear at any goddamn moment, I'd tackle him to the ground, but we both step back like the sensible parents we are.

"I have something I want to show you, too," he says.

47

I lead her back to my house and tell her to wait in the living room while I run upstairs and come back downstairs with my Lucy journal.

I open the journal to after we met at Maeve's. I hold it out so she can read it for herself. There's no entry for that night, because I got home too late and was too tired and (still) horny for her to write in the journal. Anyway, it's not that night I'd want her to see, but all the nights following it. "Look."

The entries after the night I met her at Maeve's are all dated and addressed to Lucy but blank—until the very last entry.

"I couldn't," I explain. "I tried to write to her again after the night we met, but I couldn't make myself do it. I'd get the date down, and my greeting to her, and then—nothing."

Her gaze flashes to mine, confusion written there.

"Because I knew everything had changed. I knew meeting you had changed everything, and I didn't want to tell her."

"Oh," she says. "Oh."

Her eyes are huge. She bites her lip.

"And then I moved in next door and it was even more true. I mean, maybe I didn't know consciously, but some part of me must have known, because I couldn't write to Lucy. Until the Friday night before the wedding." I push the journal closer. "Read it."

She hesitates. I can't blame her. I don't think many women would want to read what their lover had written to his dead wife—at least not any more than she's already had to stomach. But I don't think I can make her believe—*really* believe—unless she sees it for herself.

"That's the entry I saw," she says.

"I know."

She drops her chin and studies the page. I read over her shoulder.

Dear Lucy,

I love you. I will probably always love you.

I have something I have to tell you, though. I met someone, and I'm going away this weekend with her. Her name is Elle. I don't know exactly what's going to happen, but I think it could be something real. Something serious. I'm sorry I didn't tell you sooner, but it felt—weird and awkward. I hope wherever you are, you don't have weird and awkward, and you get what I'm trying to say. Thanks for listening.

Love,

Sawyer

She looks up at me. Whispers, "I thought—"

"I know. I get it."

"I'm so sorry. I only read the first line. And then I freaked out and my brain went blank and all the words blurred together."

"I figured."

"I'm an idiot."

"Nah," I say. "You just have a little PTSD because your ex-husband is an asshole."

That makes her smile.

I reach toward the night table and grab a pen. "Hey. Can I do something?"

Her eyes are quizzical.

"I want to write one last entry. I want to say goodbye to her."

Her eyes open wide, and she bites her lip. "You don't have to do that—"

"I don't have to. But I want to."

"Are you sure? I don't have to watch—you could do it in private?"

"I want you to. If that's okay with you."

She nods, her face very serious.

I begin writing as she watches over my shoulder.

Dear Lucy,

I love you. I will probably always love you.

But it's time for me to stop writing to you. Because of Elle. Because I'm crazy about her, Luce. Crazy. I'm head over heels in love with her. And I think there's a chance if I run with it, we could be really, really good together. With the boys, too. A family.

So—there you have it. I hope you meant what you said about wanting me to be happy, because I don't seem to be able to help it when I'm around her.

And I can't write to you anymore because I need to give Elle this part of me now. All the things I've been telling you, I need to—I want to—tell her. So I'm saying goodbye. Again. I guess this is a bigger kind of goodbye than the one we said before. Or maybe just different? What do I know?

I love you. I'll probably always love you. Goodbye, Luce.

Love, Sawyer

"Oh, Jesus, Elle, don't cry," I say, which is a ridiculous thing to say for so many reasons, not the least of which is that my own vision is blurred.

"I can't help it," she moans, her beautiful face streaked with tears. "I just have all these feelings. And they're all mixed up. I mean, how can I want her to be alive and with you and Jonah and still be so glad she's not here so you can be with me? How can I feel so bad for both of you and so happy for both of *us,* especially when those two overlap?"

"I don't know," I say, because, shit, I really don't. "If I knew the answer to that—hell, I don't know how I can be so sad and happy at the same time, either, but apparently it's possible. And most of the time, to be perfectly honest, with the exception of these last few weeks, which have sucked, because I've missed you so fucking much, I'm just happy. Happy that you're in the world, happy that you live next door, happy that you own those ridiculous rubber-duck pajamas and that goofy apron—"

She hug-tackles me.

"Me, too. Happy. And I'm in love with you, too. I love you."

"I love you."

I reach a hand out and cup her chin. Then we're kissing again.

A long time passes before we come up for air.

"What will you do while we're gone?"

Jonah asks this in a tone of utter innocence that both cracks me up and breaks my heart. Kids, I tell you. Not too long from now—four years? five?—everything will be loaded with double meanings as their focus shifts from tag and board games to the hormones destroying their equilibrium, but for right now, Jonah's polite inquiry means exactly what he says:

What are you and my dad going to do with yourselves while Madden and I are at camp? What do parents do without their children to entertain them and provide them with meaningful caretaking tasks?

Beside me, in the driver's seat, Sawyer is waging an epic battle against laughter; I can feel his body shaking. One month after our (earth-moving) makeup, we're in my car together en route to drop-off for the outdoor adventure camp. The boys' stuff is jammed into the trunk, and the boys themselves are squirming with excitement and anticipation in the backseat. As we pull up to the drop-off spot—the parking lot outside Mountainwear—I put on my best flight attendant voice and remind them to obey the "fasten seatbelt" sign until the vehicle has come to a complete stop and the driver has turned off the sign.

Needless to say, the instant the car comes to a stop, they are both out of their seatbelts and out the doors, racing toward the trip leaders. Because what is better in life than a chance to spend five days with a bunch of other pre-teens, enjoying the great outdoors?

The chance to be home alone without any kids around at all.

Just saying.

We follow the boys out of the car, grabbing their stuff from the trunk, and drop it off. We listen to the trip leaders' eloquently delivered speech about camper behavior and what will cause campers to get sent home ("Our boys will be fine unless someone's gender identity gets stepped on," I whisper to Sawyer), and then we hug and kiss the boys goodbye and head back to the car.

The boys kinda sorta know what's going on. They know that Sawyer and I made up our "fight" and that we're back to being friends. I think they might sort of suspect, in an innocent way, that we're "special friends." But even though Sawyer and I are pretty sure marriage is in our future (and probably our near future), we also think it's a good idea to keep things simple for the boys until we make a public commitment. So we're holding on to both houses, we're spending the middle of the night in our own beds . . . I'm not complaining. It's been blissful.

But this week? Just the two of us? A whole week of sharing a house and a shower and a bed?

Super. Huge. Special. Treat.

Which is why, as we pull away from our offspring, neither of us is dwelling too much on how this is the boys' first time away from home, or how much we'll miss them, or even if they're in good hands.

"You know what I'm most looking forward to?" Sawyer asks. "Aside from waking you up in the middle of the night by going down on you."

I make a small desperate noise, and he laughs.

"Drive faster," I instruct.

But he doesn't appear to be heading home.

"Where are you—?"

"Patience, grasshopper," he says.

I give him a hard time (and I do mean hard, regaling him with all the things I could be doing to him if we were at home by ourselves right now) for the duration of the trip, until I realize: we're headed to Maeve's.

"Did you know they do a mean brunch?"

"I didn't," I say.

He gets us two seats at the new bar. It's not quite like the old one, but I'm okay with that, because Sawyer is turning the old bar into a big, circular table that's perfect for family game night.

Maeve's new decor is, well, *just* like the old decor, and that's as it should be.

"Two mimosas," Sawyer tells the bartender. "And brunch menus, please."

"Are we . . . celebrating something?" I ask.

"You never answered my question."

"What question?"

"'You know what I'm most looking forward to?'"

I laugh. "Oh, right. You distracted me before I could answer."

"I'm looking forward to falling asleep with you in my arms."

"Ah, me too. Too bad it's only four nights."

"So that's the thing, Elle."

He's fumbling with something in his pocket, and all of a sudden, my hands and feet go cold, and my heart starts pounding—in the best possible way.

The bartender sets the mimosas on the bar in front of us, but we both ignore them. I'm too busy looking into Sawyer's dark, intense eyes, and he's looking back, but this time I *know* what the expression is there, it's love and trust and devotion, and he opens the little velvet box in his hand and holds it out to me.

"I know it's fast. But I also know that life is short, and I know how I feel. I want us to be a family. I want the boys to be brothers. And I want to fall asleep with you in my arms, not just for the next four nights, but every night for the rest of our lives. Elle Dunning, will you marry me?"

I look at his beloved face, the eyes that still hold a hint of grief but also so much joy and lust for life, and I don't have to think about it at all.

"Oh, Sawyer. Yes. Yes, yes, yes!"

He takes the ring from the box and slides it on my finger. Applause breaks out—the bartender is clapping and so are a lot of other people in the restaurant. I feel like clapping myself, but instead I examine the ring on my finger—it's a solitaire, round diamond. Restrained and eloquent, like Sawyer.

"Kiss me?" I whisper.

"You remember what happened last time?" he murmurs.

As it turns out, neither of us is that hungry. Shame about those mimosas going to waste, though . . .

Since it's daylight, we do the rest of Maeve's patrons, and ourselves, the favor of getting ourselves home before he kisses me.

EPILOGUE

MANY MONTHS LATER—SAWYER

"Strip club," Jack says.

Brooks has called a meeting of our friends and invited them to weigh in on the subject of my rapidly approaching, still-unplanned bachelor party.

The sun is out, so instead of holing up in our favorite bar, we're sprawled on a patch of lawn at the construction site where Jack's currently working.

"Don't be ridiculous," Brooks says. "Sawyer repurposes old lumber to sell high-end furniture. He doesn't want his bachelor party at a strip club."

I really, really don't want to ask Brooks what the connection is between those two thoughts, so I just let his observation stand. It's true: I don't want my bachelor party at a strip club.

"What about Vegas?" Brooks asks.

Chase snorts. "He's not the strip club type, but Vegas is where your mind goes?"

The longer I know Chase, the more he grows on me.

"Doesn't everyone love Vegas?" Jack asks—unironically, I think, which is the best thing about Jack.

"I don't," I say. "Also, I want to include Madden and Jonah. So there's that."

The boys were ecstatic, of course, to hear that Elle and I were planning to get married. We told them they can have a special part in the ceremony to commemorate officially becoming brothers, and they've been hard at work writing their vows. There's a line in there about taking turns with the better Xbox controller.

Eve is working on finding a buyer for the house Jonah and I have been living in, and meanwhile, I'm putting the finishing touches on the house's bathrooms and finally getting around to the exterior painting and roofing projects. But of course I'm leaving myself enough time for furniture-building—the catalog pieces are selling as fast as I can construct them, and I'm loving the extra income. What with the furniture money and Elle's advance on *Splitsville,* we've added lots of new board games to our collection and promised the boys a fun family vacation after the honeymoon.

The wedding planning is on track, Elle and her mom are having a blast and staying surprisingly chill about it all. Pretty much all that's left is this bachelor party question.

I was hoping if I ignored it long enough it would go away, but I wasn't giving my brother nearly enough credit. Or way too much.

"What about a camping trip?"

That piece of genuine brilliance comes, of course, from Chase.

"Yes," I say.

They all look at me.

"That's what I want to do."

Brooks's eyebrows go way up. "You want to spend your last nights of freedom—"

"Spoken like a man who has not yet discovered the joys of cohabitation," Jack murmurs.

"—in smelly clothes in the woods?"

"Yup."

"Okay, then," Brooks says, because he is many things, but above all, he is a very supportive brother, and I love the shit out of him. He already has his phone out. "I'm gonna see if Big Gabe can do something for us."

Big Gabe is what we call Brooks' and my friend Gabe Wilder, to distinguish him from Little Gabe, who is Jack's son. Big Gabe runs a wilderness adventuring company in Central Oregon, in the town of Rush Creek, where Brooks and I grew up.

"Hey!" Brooks says into the phone. "How are things in the Wilder world?"

He's silent for a long time. A very long time. His forehead wrinkles. His eyebrows go up. Chase gives me a worried look. In addition to being an old friend to Brooks and me, Gabe's also one of Chase's first and best business partners. Anything that goes wrong in Gabe's world affects Chase's.

"Okay," Brooks says finally. And then, after another pause, "Yeah. Listen. I did have a question for you, but I think you have enough on your plate. We'll plan a trip to Rush Creek to hang with you guys when things calm down."

When Brooks sets the phone down, Chase says, "He can't help?"

Brooks shakes his head slowly. "Big Gabe's mom hired

some fancy New York City consultant to revamp Wilder Adventures to pull in all the new spa-and-wedding business that Rush Creek has attracted the last couple of years. Apparently this consultant wants Wilder Adventures to become Wilder *Romantic* Adventures."

"Oh, shit," Chase says. "That's a *lot* of rebranding." He pulls out his phone and sends a text—probably to Liv, who deals with most of the branded clothing lines.

"How does Gabe feel about all this?" I ask.

"Well, that's the thing," Brooks says. "Gabe's totally opposed."

I raise an eyebrow. "Oh, that sounds fun."

"No," Brooks says, and gets a look on his face I've come to recognize. It's the look of a man who knows one of his compatriots is about to get himself into a whole world of trouble—and who's eagerly anticipating the show. "Here's the fun part. This consultant is drop dead gorgeous. And smoking hot. And she's living above Gabe's office and showering in his house."

I grin, and so do Chase and Jack. Because all three of us know from personal experience what happens when two opposites find themselves under one roof—even for a few minutes a day.

I shrug and cross my arms, still smiling.

"Guess I'll have to plan my own damn camping trip."

ACKNOWLEDGMENTS

Do Over, *Head Over Heels*, and *Sleepover* were first published in 2018. But re-releasing a book is its own special kind of project, and I have many people to thank with their help in making this edition possible!

First of all, many thanks to my readers for always being along for the ride! I do this for you, and I'm so grateful every time I get an email, message, or smoke signal from the ether telling me these characters have meant as much to you as they have to me.

Mr. Bell and our kids usually get the last place in my acknowledgments, which isn't fair at all, because they have first place in my heart. They're unfailingly patient and supportive and in every way the best family an author—or anyone—could want. I love you all so much.

Thank you so much to Kate Davies and Jessica Auerbach (aka my mom!) for being my awesome readers this time around! Thank you for taking time away from your own work to help make this book the best it could be.

Huge thanks also to the author friends who support me on a regular basis—Dylann Crush, Megan Ryder, Christina

Hovland, Brenda St. John Brown, Claire Marti, Christine D'Abo, Gwen Hernandez, Rachel Grant, Kate, Kris Kennedy, Karen Booth, Susannah Nix, Stina Lindenblatt, and many, many more, including but not limited to the authors of the Girls' Night In Book Club, the Corner of Smart and Sexy, Small Town World Domination, Wide for the Win, Tinsel and Tatas, and the RAM Rom-Com group.

Thank you to my agent, Emily Sylvan Kim, and my sub rights agent, Tina Shen, who work to make things happen for me behind the scenes!

I cannot imagine doing any of my jobs without the love and support of my amazing friends, Aimee, Chelsea, Cheryl, Darya, Ellen, Gail, Jess, Julia, Kathy, Lauren, Molly, Soomie, and Tracey. Love you!

ALSO BY SERENA BELL

Wilder Adventures

Make Me Wilder

Walk on the Wilder Side

Wilder With You

A Little Wilder

Returning Home

Hold On Tight

Can't Hold Back

To Have and to Hold

Holding Out

Tierney Bay

So Close

So True

Under One Roof

Do Over

Head Over Heels

Sleepover

New York Glitz

Still So Hot!

Hot & Bothered

Standalone

Turn Up the Heat

ABOUT THE AUTHOR

USA Today bestselling author Serena Bell writes contemporary romance with heat, heart, and humor. A former journalist, Serena has always believed that everyone has an amazing story to tell if you listen carefully, and you can often find her scribbling in her tiny garret office, main-lining chocolate and bringing to life the tales in her head.

Serena's books have earned many honors, including a RITA finalist spot, an RT Reviewers' Choice Award, Apple Books Best Book of the Month, and Amazon Best Book of the Year for Romance.

When not writing, Serena loves to spend time with her college-sweetheart husband and two hilarious kiddos—all of whom are incredibly tolerant not just of Serena's imaginary friends but also of how often she changes her hobbies and how passionately she embraces the new ones. These days, it's stand-up paddle boarding, board-gaming, meditation, and long walks with good friends.